Grandfather Speaks Again

Books by Bob Anderson

Sarge, What Now?
Anderson Rules
Grandfather Speaks

TAC Leader Series
#1 What Honor Requires
#2 Night Hawks
#3 Retribution

**Books by Jerry Ahern,
Sharon Ahern and Bob Anderson**

The Survivalist Series
#30 The Inheritors of the Earth
#31 Earth Shine
#32 The Quisling Covenant
#33 Deep Star
#34 Lodestar

The Rourke Chronicles
#1 Everyman

Short Stories
Shades of Love
Once Upon a Time
Light Dreams

Grandfather Speaks Again

Bob Anderson

SPEAKING VOLUMES, LLC
NAPLES, FLORIDA
2016

Grandfather Speaks Again

Copyright © 2015 by Bob Anderson
Edited by Pamela Anderson

ISBN 978-1-62815-490-0

Many people have come into my life at interesting times to teach me something and then leave. As I heard it said, some came for a reason, some came for a season and some came forever. I was always glad to see them come; sometimes I was glad to see them go. Sometimes I was really glad. But when they left they took a part of me, and in that taking, they left part of themselves. That part lives in a special place within my heart and memories.

Hopefully this book will draw some of us back together; at least for a moment or two. Most are still alive, but again... like leaves on a tree, we have been scattered by the winds of time. Thank you for having touched my life. Thank you for the teachings you gave me.

This book is dedicated to those who
left and never came back.
To Mongo who did.
To Dogman and Top Eye who never left.
To Mike Spinella who showed up and
to George King, my Wizard.
To Woodrow Call and Gus McCrae
who understood friendship.
Damn few do.

Grandfather Speaks
and
Grandfather Speaks Again
are books that inspire, educate, motivate
and help find guidance in unexpected ways, to
anyone walking the path of their lives.

If I can throw a single ray of light,
Across the darkened pathway of another;
If I can aid some soul to clearer sight
Of light and duty and thus bless my brother;
If I can wipe from any human cheek a tear
I shall not have, then, lived in vain while here.
If I can guide some erring to truth
Inspire within his heart a sense of duty;
If I can plant within the soul of a rosy plant
A sense of light, a love of truth and beauty;
If I can teach one man that God and Heaven
are near;
I shall not have, then, lived in vain while here.
If from my mind I can banish doubt and fear
And keep my life attuned to truth, love
and kindness;
If I can scatter light and hope and cheer
And help and remove the curse of
mental blindness;
If I can make joy more, more hope, less pain
I shall not have, lived in vain while here.
If by life's road side I can plant a tree
Beneath whose shade some wearied
head may rest
Though I may never share its shade or see

Its beauty I shall yet be truly blessed
Though no one knows my name.
—Anonymous

∞∞∞∞∞∞∞∞∞∞∞

Selfishness is not living as one wishes to live,
it is asking others to live as one wishes to live.
—Oscar Wilde

∞∞∞∞∞∞∞∞∞∞∞

Caring was the only thing I ever did when we were friends. The minute you turned your back was the minute I realized I deserved better. I have found that moving on is simple; what you leave behind, that makes it difficult. I also found that sometimes you have to give up on people. Not because you don't care, but because they don't.
It's tough when your friend begins to ignore you. It's even tougher to pretend you don't mind. It breaks my heart to see the person who I thought was my best friend, forget about me, lie to me, ignore me and just leave me alone without a warning. You were the one I thought who wouldn't...let me down. What shocked me is...when I needed you the most to do what you said you would do... what you said you wanted to do... you were the first to walk away.
—Author unknown

Introduction

Hi there; come up on the deck with me. Pretty view, isn't it? The woods on the other side of the lake... the lake used to be a lot bigger. Oops, I'm sorry... take a seat. The weather is pretty nice today but I did set a little fire in the chiminea, kinda cut the chill a little, you know, if we need it. The breeze can get stiff out here. There's another glass on the patio table, if you would like something to drink. I don't know if you smoke but if you want to... go ahead. It is up to you.

When I started this story, it was about lost friendships. Now that I've I finished it, it still is... sort of. But, it's more about magic—the fingerprint of God!

Back then I was bothered because another of my strongest friendships had failed. Not just a casual friendship, but a really significant one—more of a brother than a friend. It had lasted almost forty years; that is the kind of friendship I am talking about. It made no sense to me. Still doesn't.

I needed to find some sense... make some sense out of it. It just sort of happened... unbidden.

Grandfather came back to me and he took me

back to places and people I knew long ago. I went back to my heroes, "The good guys."

As Grandfather says, ***These have been your truest friends—your heroes, my son.***

You see, it ain't easy being my friend. That's because I expect... No, actually, I require things from my friends. I require the things I give to them to be returned. Things like honor, honesty, camaraderie, compassion, passion, strength and sacrifice—these are things some folks can't (or won't) give.

Good people fall and fail—then they get up and try again. Good people make mistakes and hurt others—then they learn from their mistakes and TRY not to make them again. Good people find themselves in position where there is no "operator's manual"—so they write one.

I realized that many of my truest friends were fictional. Great teachers, great role models; steadfast and true. They are always there, always valiant and more REAL than some of the humans I know. I like that about them. After all Richard Bach once said, "If you will practice being fictional for a while, you will understand that fictional characters are sometimes more real than people with bodies and heartbeats."

In the end, I've come to realize the essence of my lost friendships really only existed in my mind;

not in the hearts of those "friends." That realization was hard to accept; but being hard to accept did not lessen the validity of the statement or the sense of loss that I felt.

I found along the way the magic was that sometimes friendships are not really lost; just misplaced. Other times, they are not lost; they are destroyed. What is the difference?

One is permanent (I think) the other is not (I think). The problem is I don't have the power or the insight to know the difference. Every man can be filled with doubt from time to time; I suspect the same is true of every woman. Each of us has "suffering the slings and arrows" of those that understand less, feel less, do less and (in my never to be humble opinion) are less. I couldn't afford to lose any more friends so I started a quest to make some sense out of what had happened.

Now, sit back and let me tell you what happened, how it happened and what I figured out when I went back to my heroes. Why? Simple, if it hasn't happened to you... it probably will. Maybe my story will help you a little bit. Hope so...

Chapter One

Here is how it all started:

My wife, Pam, and I have a home in southwest Missouri. We used to have a two and a half acre lake behind our home but a leak developed in the overflow drain pipe and drained my two and a half acre lake down to a fifty foot pond.

You have probably had those periods where it didn't make any difference what you were doing... nothing seemed to work. No matter how simple the problem... it became more complicated than it needed to be... it took longer to fix and cost more than you had budgeted. Nothing really earth shattering, just a seemingly continuing pile of irritations, distractions and delays. Nothing more than an irritation.

[**irritation, a noun**. The state of feeling annoyed, impatient, or angry. Annoyance, exasperation, vexation, indignation, impatience, crossness, displeasure, chagrin, pique; anger, rage, fury, wrath, aggravation; irritant, annoyance, thorn in my

side/flesh, bother, trial, torment, plague, inconvenience, nuisance, aggravation, pain in the
neck.][1]

The lake is still too deep to repair, but does allow us to watch the deer and turkeys come down
to drink. I still miss my lake though. Once it
seemed as if God had plugged the hole in the pipe,
but it did not hold and I decided it would be a "next
year" project. Nothing more than an irritation.

Not long ago, I had a blow up with a good friend.
At the time of this writing, we are "sniffing each
other" out to see if the relationship can be sal-
vaged. Both of us feel we were in the right. Nothing more than an irritation.

There have been other irritations. Writing was
going well again after a four-month hiatus. Pam
was closing on us releasing four books by the end
of the year. Several projects associated with the
writings had been delayed. Nothing really earth
shattering, just a seemingly continuing pile of irritations, distractions and delays. Nothing more
than irritations.

I had made an investment over a year ago.
"Hey, there is really good potential here," I was
told. Well, it had gone nowhere, although there
had been a lot of activity... dreams, goals to "fix"

problems in the world, opportunities to "pay it forward"... nothing had been accomplished. Nothing more than an irritation.

Only one project had come to a welcomed end. Two years ago I had set out to restore an electric Commuta Car; you may remember seeing them on the highways during the late seventies through the early nineties. Mine was red in color and my first thought was to paint it gray with the numbers NCC 1701 across the hood. I thought to make it look like a shuttle craft complete with fake engine nacelles and a sound system with Star Trek sound effects. I wanted to drive past our local City Hall and blast them with phasers and photon torpedoes.

[**perversity, a noun.** A deliberate desire to behave in an unreasonable or unacceptable way; contrariness.][2]

In any event, I did not know enough about D.C. electronics to complete the project and for two years the thing simply occupied space in my barn. My wife put it on Craig's list and it was sold in less than a week; to an electrician of all people. When he picked it up we asked him to take a look at one of our house circuits that had been malfunctioning. In the closing of that project, I created a problem.

The electrician didn't know nearly as much about electricity as he thought he did. That began a week of confusion and a total loss of electricity that lasted three days.

To make a long and irritating story a little shorter, by the end of that episode we had to dig up the driveway, and spend over $1,200 just to get back to where we had been—almost. In the process, we fried two ceiling fans, the control panel for the oven, two banks of ceiling lights and the hot tub. It had to be rewired.

Four electrical wall outlets and a lighting fixture—the original problem—still didn't work. Winter came early in Southwest Missouri and the temperature had dropped to the teens. Thank goodness for propane. Oh, and we lost my computer and home phone... For a writer the computer is essential. Luckily, Pam's laptop wasn't affected and our production schedule was able to continue with only minor issues. The worse part was we lost electricity twenty minutes before a new episode of NCIS was to air.

I love Leroy Jethro Gibbs and his crew.

Seven days into the process, we were still trying to get things back to normal. Problem was, we still weren't sure what the total cost was going to be or how long it would take to get things back to where they had been, with improvements.

But it was only an irritation.

[**irritation, a noun**. The state of feeling annoyed, impatient, or angry. Annoyance, exasperation, vexation, indignation, impatience, crossness, displeasure, chagrin, pique; anger, rage, fury, wrath, aggravation; irritant, annoyance, thorn in my side/flesh, bother, trial, torment, plague, inconvenience, nuisance, aggravation, pain in the neck.][3]

Or in my case, pain in the butt, headache, burr under my saddle.

These and several other issues were weighing heavily on me and keeping me off balance a bit; especially the blow up with my friend. You have probably had those periods where it didn't make any difference what you were doing... nothing seemed to work. No matter how simple the problem... it became more complicated than it needed to be... it took longer to fix and cost more than you had budgeted. Nothing really earth shattering, just a seemingly continuing pile of irritations, distractions and delays. Then you have a fight with a friend...

Oh, and we had family coming to stay with us for Thanksgiving in less than two weeks.

∞∞∞∞∞∞∞∞∞∞

"And God is able to make all grace abound to you, so that in all things at all times, having all that you need, you will abound in every good work."[4]

Chapter Two

It was a Saturday night. Pam had gone to bed early and I was watching an old western on TV. We had finally gotten the hot tub functional and it had soothed my sore muscles, not to mention my frayed nerves. Hours of spreading dirt and surface gravel with my small tractor to hide the damage done to our driveway during the electrical repairs, had taken its toll on my back. I have a back blade but no front-end loader. It took five or six hours of attacking a four-foot high, twelve-foot long pile of gravel.

I must have dosed off in the recliner. Then reality went spontaneous on me.

[**spontaneous, an adjective**. Results coming or resulting from a natural impulse or tendency; without effort or premeditation; natural and unconstrained; unplanned: for example a spontaneous burst of applause or a person given to acting upon sudden impulses... or a natural phenomena arising from internal forces or causes; independent of external agencies; self-acting...][1]

A sound drifted into my dream; a steady drum beat, THUMP... THUMP... THUMP, THUMP, THUMP... THUMP? I stirred and glanced out the double doors in the living room. Something... something did not look right and I got up. There was light flickering on the remaining few leaves of the trees beside the house. *Crap... something is on fire,* was my first thought. *Probably left over electrical problems.* I grabbed a coat, a flashlight, a pistol and charged to the front door and jerked it open, ready to shout "FIRE" and tear Pam from her sleep.

Something was burning, but there was no smoke.

I walked around the house to where the lake used to be. The drum beat continued. I saw the fire. Not a rampant blaze but a significant campfire. On the far side of the now dry lake bed are two large boulders—underwater when the lake is full, now on dry land. In front of them, the campfire burned. I moved the flashlight around, but saw no one...

No smoke, no smell of something burning. The drumming continued... The scene was strangely familiar; I knew that campfire... I remembered it from Grandfather's visit several years ago. I stood amazed, excited.

I shoved the pistol into the belt of my jeans, and using the flashlight I threaded my way through the brush down to the lake bed. I crossed the little stream that runs into the lake/pond; now frozen solid. I approached the campfire and called out, "Hello the camp!"

A voice came out of the darkness, *Come sit with me. We will make talk, we will make smoke. There is much to learn.*

"Grandfather, is it you?"

Who else would it be my son?

"I didn't expect to see you again, I was afraid you had died."

How can I die? At our last meeting the time came for me to leave. Now it is time for me to come back. I felt your need of me.

He came out of the shadows, still wearing a buckskin shirt and breeches with moccasins and a simple headband, also of buckskin. The shirt was laced and had natural dyes that had been applied in patterns. He had spread a blanket on the big rock and pointed to the smaller boulder. He said, *Come, sit with me. We will make talk, we will make smoke. There is much to learn.*

He still reminded me of the great Native American character actor of the 1980's, Chief Dan George. Then there was the fire. The sticks and branches were stacked into a pyramid and I noticed one had a curious knot that reminded me of a face looking back from the fire. It had been in the first campfire we had shared... how long ago?

I couldn't remember. I said, "You are here, with me."

Where else would I be. We came here together you and I because it is where we're supposed to be.

"Why are you here? I mean, why now?"

To talk, to make smoke, to learn. Talk about all things, smoke the pipe and there is everything to learn. Sit.

Only moments before the chill of the night had gone through my clothes and my boots. My ears and face had stung with it. Now the campfire chased the chill away and I was as warm as I had been in the house. "It is good to see you Grandfather. I have missed you, especially the last few months."

How can that be? he said. *I am with you always, you just do not see me or hear me. That is because you do not look or listen.*

"But I think of you almost every day."

Ah, so that is the problem, you are thinking too much and doing too little.

He pulled a buck skin bag from off his shoulder and removed his pipe. The long wooden stem was decorated with horse hair, feathers and carvings; the stem was carved from red pipestone.

He packed the bowl from another small leather bag and reached into the fire for a burning twig.

He took several puffs to get it going and then stood and raised the pipe to the four points of a compass.

"It has been too long since we sat by the fire, Grandfather."

Not too long, not too soon. It is time now, that is all. What you call Time, I call Life. But it is a white man's wish to control life and time, bending them to your own desires. It was man that created Time, the Great Spirit created Life. It was man who began measuring it; locking it into minutes and hours and days and weeks and months and years. The Great Spirit only created seasons so we would know when to plant and when the buffalo would return.

Your people began to measure Time and try to bend it and Life to your desires. What about the desires of Time and Life? Do these not count more than yours?

"How can time and life have desires? Those are things without thoughts or consciousness. How can they desire?" I asked him.

Yes, I see it is time for us to speak again. You have forgotten much, or you never knew much... Thoughts and Consciousness... Only man then can have desires? Only man is alive? Only man can think and be aware? Are these what you believe?

11

∞∞∞∞∞∞∞∞∞∞

"Peace is the number one beautiful ornament you can wear, I really believe that.

They say you should always wear a smile, but I don't believe that you should 'always' wear a smile, seriously, you're going to look stupid! But peace, you should always carry peace within you, it's the most beautifying thing you could ever have or do. Peace makes your heart beautiful and it makes you look beautiful, too. You want to have perfect physical posture when you stand, sit, and walk, and peace is the perfect posture of the soul, really. Try perfect posture outside as well as inside. Peace creates grace and grace gives peace."[2]

Chapter Three

"Honestly, I don't know what I believe anymore," I said seriously. "Every time I put my faith in someone or get excited about a project... Well, it just doesn't seem I have the power to make it work."

Very good, that is important to realize. It is possible you are not as lost as I fear. Power comes from the Great Spirit, our Great Father. Sometimes he will loan some to a man but that man must use it correctly, for a proper purpose, with a smiling heart and he can fly like the eagle, or... the Great Father will take it back and let the man crash to the prairie.

But what you call Time and what I call Life do have desires... In both of our worlds, it is the desire that you learn what you can when you can. Your Time and my Life cannot be rushed or controlled.

"What do you mean?"

In the spring the flowers grow, the buffalo come back. Why? To use your word, it is Time for them. To use my word, it is Life following its desire.

"So Time and Life have desires, they have consciousness?"

Not as man does, they simply ARE. IS, is always more powerful than could be or should be. IS, is... what is more powerful than that?

"But... as a man I only have so much time to accomplish what I'm trying to do."

Who cares what you are trying to do, except you? The winter does not care, the trees do not care, the eagle does not care. Only man cares and because he cares, because he wants, because he seeks, because he tries to control all things to make happen what he wishes... the Great Father—the Great Spirit—will let the man crash to the prairie to teach him the lesson of humility.

"Well... well, that sucks. That's not fair!"

Fair, this word means what? Does it mean that which you seek is good and when you receive what you sought... that is fair?

"Well, yes. I guess that is what it means."

So you know better than the Great Spirit? You know when the buffalo should come, when the flowers should bloom. What of the cycle of life? Fire must come to the plains and to the forests so the grasses and trees are cleansed and become stronger.

Rain must fall, but floods will happen—each has a purpose. As it is in nature, it is with man. If you only receive what you seek, how then can you grow and learn.

The Great Father is a teacher. You are the student. He must teach, you must learn or the cycle cannot be complete. He knows more than you. He knows you are capable of more than you think.

Man thinks with his mind, the Great Father needs not to think... because he knows. Tell me my son, after your greatest failures... have you not been stronger? Have you not been smarter? Have you not been better than before?

"Well... yes."

Would you have sought those failures on your own?

"Of course not. That would have been stupid. I didn't want those problems. I didn't want the pain, the hurt... or the effort."

Of course not, you are a man. You are the student, HE is the teacher. HE knew that you needed to learn. HE knew you needed to grow. And... HE knew you were strong enough to do both. You did not.

∞∞∞∞∞∞∞∞∞∞∞∞∞

"It is the tenderness that breaks our hearts. The

loveliness that leaves us stranded on the shore, watching the boats sail away. It is the sweetness that makes us want to reach out and touch the soft skin of another person. And it is the grace that comes to us, undeserving though we may be."[1]

Chapter Four

"Well, damn it. There are things that I can do that would make things better," I bristled, "because I have something important to say with my books, with my projects. I want to help people learn from them, to be better because of them."

Grandfather chuckled. **What do you have to say that has not been said before? Nothing. What do you think that has not been thought before? Nothing. My son, you are a good man... but you are not the best man. It is not your place to MAKE things happen. It is your place to LET them happen. This is particularly true in dealing with other people.**

"So I have to let people screw me? I have to let people lie to me? I have to let other people mess up what I'm trying to do? I have to let them NOT do what they say they are going to do... what they said they wanted to do?"

No, you do not. If you do not trust someone, do not walk with them. Leave them and go your own way. If you do trust someone, consider that what you say they do to you, you may be doing to them. Are you not trying to make them like you? To think like you, to work

like you? They are not like you... they are like them. Would you want to be them?

"Of course not," I said in righteous indignation. "It is just that people don't say what they mean, they don't do what they say. That is no way to live!"

Were you not like that at one time?

"Sure, but I changed."

Did you? He held up one finger and said, *We teach best what we most need to learn.*[1] He held up a second finger and said, *What we hate most in others is what we fear most in ourselves.*[2] He closed his hand and took a deep lungful of smoke from the pipe, slowly letting it out. *You are a good man but you are not the best man. Think of three people that have wronged you— remember I know your thoughts. One of them you wronged, though you did not do it with malice. One of them you trusted and should not have but you believed in him instead of believing in yourself. The last you tried to remake when he did not truly wish to change. He could not. Is it not so?*

"But in our last visit, you told me there is something called magic," I finally said.

Magic is real. I told you that you do not understand you already have all of the magic any man may possess. You think that because you see what is wrong with the world, it needs to be changed.

Like the magpie, we see something shiny and we want it. We don't know why we want it, we just do. It is much like the dog chasing the car, what would he do if he caught it.

Man is like the dog and the magpie. We collect shiny things that have no meaning. We pursue what we cannot catch; and if we did, we would have no use of it. People talk of seeking success and happiness.

Too often man seeks a goal with no more understanding of that goal than a gopher has. Men do not study success or happiness. They only see that it is shiny or that it is in motion and they launch off in pursuit of it. You do not understand the Great Spirit's plan.

Time and Life and magic simply are. They cannot be controlled. You are trying to control the magic; and that, my son, does not work.

Since you think you have no true friends, I will let you 'borrow' some of mine.

∞∞∞∞∞∞∞∞∞∞

*"I can tell you that you will have
your hearts broken more by
the people you love than*

19

Bob Anderson

by the people you hate.
But you must still dare to love.
The rewards are worth far
more than the risks."[3]

Chapter Five

I remember thinking I wasn't sure what Grand-father meant. I suspect that the strength of friend-ships is always being tested; at least they have been for me. Someone once said, "If your friend-ship lasts, you'll know more about your friend. And if it doesn't last, you'll know more about yourself." I guess that is a fair trade off, but an expensive one.

Sometimes, I may like you but we may not be friends. I may respect you but we may not be friends. To be friends, it takes both. I do not ex-pect you to be perfect; I'm not. And on that basis we can suit each other admirably, as long as there is mutual respect. Respect is a big deal for people, at least for me.

Once, in the mid-eighties, I was hired as a Quality Control Supervisor. The big boss intro-duced me to my boss, telling him I had a college degree. Bill Franklin (I changed his name) said, "Call me Bill."

He was a hard old gentleman with only a high school education; he had pulled himself up to a position of high authority and responsibility by the sweat of his own brow and determination.

A few weeks later on a Friday afternoon he called me into his office and read me the riot act. "You are the worst supervisor we ever hired. I don't know why we hired you but if you don't get on board, I'll fire you!!!"

This came as a total shock to me and I could not get him to even tell me what the problems were. Needless to say I had spent better weekends. After much thought I could only come up with one thing I could think of to change. Monday morning I made that one change.

Three weeks later, he called me back into his office and congratulated me on my wonderful transformation. Told me I was his best supervisor and when I went up for training director of the plant, he was one of my strongest supporters.

Any idea what I changed? Until the day he died, I never called him Bill again. He was always Mr. Franklin. He needed respect, he felt as though this young "whipper snapper" with a college degree wasn't showing him the proper respect, even though it was him that had set the tenure of our relationship.

[respect, a noun. A feeling of deep admiration for someone or something elicited by their abilities, qualities, or achievements. Esteem, regard, high opinion, admiration, reverence, deference, honor.

Grandfather Speaks Again

Admire (someone or something) deeply, as a result of their abilities, qualities, or achievements.][1]

∞∞∞∞∞∞∞∞∞∞

"Extraordinary afflictions are
not always the punishment
of extraordinary sins, but
sometimes the trial of
extraordinary graces."[2]

Chapter Six

I woke with a start. I was back in the living room, my coat still on the chair. My pistol and flashlight still sat on the mantle, the television was still on. Pam was still asleep. All was as it had been. I put my coat on and walked outside.

The weather was still cold, snow was trying to fall, the lake bed was dry, the stream still frozen. But there was no campfire by the two boulders; there was no Grandfather. I stood for a long moment, wondering...

I remembered what Grandfather had said long ago during one of his first visits. ***There are men you can trust; they are willing to do hard and difficult things. There are people that seek magic, although they may never climb a mountain to see the valley. There are men who strive to see the best in other men by demonstrating the best in themselves. Then there are the others... Who do you wish to walk with?***

I also remembered that reality and fiction melted together when Grandfather appeared. It was difficult to understand the difference between the two sometimes. Or was there really a difference? What was real and what was fictional? Or was it, after all... only perception?

*****

Later the next day, fog had started to roll in when a knock came to my front door. I recognized the man immediately. First of all by his size, then by his long, black western coat, the .45 on his hip and the small pillow he carried. Word was he had stolen it from a whore house in Creed, Nevada. Opening the door, I stepped out onto the deck. "Mr. Books? Mr. John Bernard Books?"

I knew Books as the gunfighter John Wayne played in his last movie "The Shootist."

Yes Sir, that's me.

"But how, you're... Well, I wasn't expecting you but I guess your visit does make sense. I understand you have what some would call a code."

You could say that, in fact I think it applies to some of your worries. My code is simple: I won't be wronged. I won't be insulted. I won't be laid a-hand on. I don't do these things to other people, and I require the same from them. Right and wrong are important, and those things are wrong.[1]

25

A friend of mine from Tennessee said, 'There's right and there's wrong. You got to do one or the other. You do the one and you're living. You do the other and you may be walking around, but you're dead as a beaver hat.'[2]

"So you understand right and wrong, respect and disrespect?"

I don't believe I ever killed a man that didn't deserve it; probably was quite a few more that deserved it but I never crossed their paths.[3]

Let's keep it simple—you've got something you need to do. Just go do it. My opinion, you've been wronged and insulted. That's two out of my three. All you need to do is figure out... what to do about it.[4]

Then he and the fog faded away.

∞∞∞∞∞∞∞∞∞∞∞∞

*"I wish grace and healing were
more abracadabra kind of things.
Also, that delicate silver bells
would ring to announce grace's
arrival. But no, it's clog and slog
and scootch, on the floor,
in the silence, in the dark."*[5]

Chapter Seven

A thought came to me. *Was I fictional?* I mean, I knew I was a real person, but was I trying to live like a fictional character. I grew up with television shows and comic books and super heroes. Comics—in those days we called them funny books.

In fact, my first job dealt with comic books. My brother, Roger, and I would collect discarded Coke bottles on the way to the local store, turn them in and get money for them.

Ah, the original days of recycling...

[**recycling, a noun or a verb.** A process to change waste materials into new products to prevent waste of potentially useful materials, reduce the consumption of fresh raw materials, reduce energy usage, reduce air pollution (from incineration) and water pollution (from land filling) by reducing the need for "conventional" waste disposal, and lower greenhouse gas emissions as compared to plastic production. Recycling is a key component of modern waste reduction and is the third component of the "Reduce, Reuse and Recycle" waste hierarchy.][1]

Roger and I bought funny books then read them and traded them. And when we were through, I'd take them up to Tommy Wilson's Barber Shop and sell them for a nickel each. That's when new funny books cost a dime... funny books and super heroes. Was I the hero in my own story? Was I trying to make others into my sidekicks? Was Batman looking for Robin? Was Robin Hood looking for Little John? Was the Lone Ranger seeking a Tonto?

I grew up watching heroes like John Wayne and Charlton Heston on the big screen. I grew up with heroes—my Dad and uncles had all fought in World War II—they were my heroes.

[**hero, a noun**. A person who is admired for their courage, outstanding achievements, or noble qualities: *a war hero.* Synonyms—brave man, champion, man of courage, great man, man of the hour, conquering hero, victor, winner, conqueror, lionheart, warrior, paladin, knight or white hat. An ideal person, paragon, exemplar, shining example, perfect example, a knight in shining armor.][2]

Heroes were real to me; they were important and still are. Maybe more important now. I was part of the same generation that tried to kill God and created the anti-hero. Maybe the problem was not that I was fictional... maybe the problem is we have lost the concept of heroes. Many of my heroes had embraced their fictional side to become something else; something... someone better.

While many younger readers might not recognize the names of these heroes, those of us of a more seasoned persuasion will. Their "fictional" selves became "reality" for us.

For example, "Fran Striker was an American writer for radio and comics, best known for creating the Lone Ranger, Green Hornet, and Sergeant Preston of the Yukon characters.

"Clayton Moore played the Lone Ranger more often than anyone else and Tonto was played by Jay Silverheels, a Mohawk from the Six Nations Indian Reserve in Ontario, Canada.[3]

"Tonto usually referred to the Lone Ranger as 'Kemo sabe,' meaning either 'faithful friend,' or 'trusty scout.' It is more likely the word derives from the Anishnaabe word, Gimoozaabi, meaning 'he looks out in secret.'[4]

"The Lone Ranger was never seen without his mask or a disguise. He always used perfect grammar and precise speech devoid of slang.

"When he was forced to use guns, he never shot to kill, but to disarm his opponent as painlessly as possible. He decided to use only silver bullets, to remind himself that life is precious and not to be thrown away.[5]

"Mr. Moore grew up in Chicago, Illinois and although his father wanted him to become a doctor, he had visions of something a little more glamorous. Naturally athletic, he practiced gymnastics during family summer vacations in Canada, eventually joining the trapeze act, The Flying Behrs, at nineteen. He had never ridden a horse before he became the Lone Ranger.[6]

"Wild Bill Elliot was born Gordon Nance in 1904 on a farm in Pattonsburg, Missouri, a small town about 60 miles northeast of Kansas City. The future 'Wild Bill Elliott' grew up around horses. His father was a commissioner at the Kansas City Stockyards and at age sixteen, Elliott won a first-place ribbon in that city's annual American Royal Horse and Livestock Show.[7]

"William Boyd, better known as Hopalong Cassidy, was your typical higher level box office Hollywood movie star of his day. Did you know he was Cecile B. De Mille's first choice for Moses in The Ten Commandments? He liked wine, and women, and enjoyed his success a little too much. One day fate dealt a nasty blow, another actor with the same name, William Boyd, was arrested during a gambling and drinking party. Boyd's career took a plunge until he became Hopalong.[8]

"Bill Boyd changed his life to be a hero for kids like me. He and his wife found a magnificent white horse. Grace named him Topper, and this is the horse Hoppy would ride up to the end of his career. The two would appear together not just in movies, but in parades and all the other personal appearances Hoppy did. After Topper died, Boyd never rode another horse.[9]

"Charles Starrett, while on the Dartmouth College football team, was hired to play a football extra in *The Quarterback*. Impressed by the job, Starrett got the acting bug and next went into vaudeville, then regional stage work and finally to Broadway.

"Bob Steele was the son of director Robert N. Bradbury. Bob Steele began his show business career early. He was part of his family's vaudeville act at age two, and toured with them all over the West Coast.[10]

"Tim Holt was born Charles John Holt III, he was given the nickname of Tim as a child. His father, Jack Holt, was 'King of the Rodeo' at the 1924 Fresno Rodeo and was accompanied by five-year-old Tim riding in the parade as the 'Crown Prince.'[11]

"Most western action film heroes begin and end their career in the saddle. Not so for cowboy idol Allan 'Rocky' Lane, who started as a leading man in major studio dramas, only to segue into 'B' serials and sagebrush sagas in later life. He later became the voice for Francis the Talking Mule.[12]

"Don 'Red' Barry went from the stage to the screen. After four years of playing villains and henchmen at various studios, Barry got the role that changed his image... Red Ryder in the Republic Pictures serial *Adventures of Red Ryder*.[13]

"Ray Corrigan was a physical culturist and very good athlete. He began working in Hollywood as a physical fitness trainer for movie stars. Bit parts in 1932 led to action roles in the *Undersea Kingdom* and *The Leathernecks Have Landed*, the same year he began his role as Tucson Smith in Republic Pictures' *Three Mesquiteers* series; he did 24 films in that series before leaving in 1939.[14]

"Sunset Carson was born with the decidedly unheroic name of Winifred Maurice Harrison. He moved to Plainview, Texas, as a boy and became a successful rodeo rider.[15]

"Singing cowboys became the rage, Monte Hale was born Samuel Buren Ely in 1919 in Ada, Oklahoma. He learned to sing and play guitar at an early age.[16]

"Jimmy Wakely was one of filmdom's last dying breed of 'B' crooning cowpokes following WWII. He had many talents such as singing, songwriting, guitar-playing, and performed in many venues—

radio, film, TV, rodeos, clubs—over his career. Eddie Dean made his name as a country-western singer on radio in the 1930s. His career started to take off in the early 1940s, though, and by 1945 he was among the more popular of the cowboy stars.[17]

"Born Marion Robert Morrison, this grandson of an American Civil War veteran, couldn't carry a tune in a saddle blanket. He swapped off the guitar but kept his six-shooter and became John Wayne.[18]

"Of the singing cowboys, the most famous were Tex Ritter, Gene Autry and of course... Roy Rogers."[19]

Then the world started changing. The cowboy ethos was replaced by "close enough for government work", "good enough to get by" and an entitlement mentality. All have set the course for a laziness that has permeated a lot further than I would have imagined.

In *Illusions: The Adventures of a Reluctant Messiah,* Richard Bach says, "... practice being fictional for a while, fictional characters are sometimes more real than people with bodies and heartbeats."

I see nothing wrong with fictional characters, I've met several. Maybe the problem was that I wasn't being fictional enough. Hmmm....

[**fiction, a noun.** The form of any work that deals, in part or in whole, with information or events that are not real, but rather, imaginary and invented by the author.][20]

I pondered, who is the author of my story? Me, of course. Much of my life has dealt with information or events that were not real, before I made them so. And making them so often involved imagination and theatrics.

Albert Einstein said, "Imagination is more important than knowledge. For knowledge is limited to all we now know and understand, while imagination embraces the entire world, and all there ever will be to know and understand."

Fortunately or unfortunately, I've always had an active imagination. Sometimes, it got me into trouble. Always, it made my life more interesting. Fiction... fact... was there really a difference?

∞∞∞∞∞∞∞∞∞∞∞

*"It is unearned love—the love that
goes before, that greets us*

Grandfather Speaks Again

*on the way. It's the help you
receive when you have no bright
ideas left, when you are empty
and desperate and have discovered
that your best thinking and most
charming charm have failed you.
Grace is the light or electricity or
juice or breeze that takes you
from that isolated place and puts
you with others who are as startled
and embarrassed and eventually
grateful as you are to be there.*"[21]

Chapter Eight

Two days later as I sat on our deck, fog started to roll in. *Strange,* I thought, *for fog to come in this late in the morning and push the sun away.* That's when I saw him, moving through the forest, rifle at the ready.

He was young, or at least had been at one time. Barely out of his teens, he had the eyes of an old man that had seen entirely too much. Dirty staff sergeant chevrons on the sleeves of his battle uniform could barely be made out. The olive drab wool was now caked with mud and dried sweat; but his rifle, an M-1 Garand, was clean and well oiled.

"Soldier," I hollered. He froze instantly on alert.

He called out, **Flash.**

I said, "Thunder" before I thought about it; the countersign worked.

You American? he asked.

"Yeah, I'm a Texan. Walk toward my voice."

He came out of the brush and looked at me. **Texan huh? Me too. Why aren't you in uniform?** His rifle still at the ready.

I thought quickly. "Special mission, can't talk about it." He nodded and relaxed, we shook hands. "Come with me," I said. "This is going to sound strange... You're..." What could I say to him?

Then it hit me, "You're back behind the lines. Safe area, come on over here." He followed me to the house and climbed up on the deck. "Sit down, take a break, we're secure here."

He removed his steel helmet and set it on the deck, squatted and sat on it the way he had ten thousand times. He moved the holstered .45 automatic on his pistol belt and leaned back against the rail.

For a moment, he just sat there with his eyes closed, relaxing for the first time in a long time. His face was streaked with dirt, a four-day beard showed. With dirty hands, he dug in his jacket pocket and produced a rumpled pack of Camels and a battered Zippo.

He offered me a Camel and I accepted. Pulling his canteen, he unscrewed the top, upending it to pour in his mouth.

CRAP, I'm empty.

"Soldier," I said. "Can I get you a drink?"

I'd appreciate it.

I stood, walked back in the house headed to the fridge. A moment later I returned and handed him a cold beer.

He took a deep draw on the bottle, downing half of it. **Damn! Man, I haven't seen one of these since I left the States.**

"How long ago was that?"

He thought. **To tell you the truth, I can't remember... My unit's been in combat most of the time, ever since we left Nancy, France. We keep heading West, always West. We were on patrol when I got separated and found your place. Seen any Krauts?** He drained the bottle.

"No Sarge, you're safe here." I looked at his unit patch. "You are 44th Infantry, right?" He nodded. "Relax. I'll get you another beer."

Thanks. Hey, do I know you, you look familiar, he called out from the deck.

Returning, I said, "No you don't, but one day we'll be pretty close. Don't worry about that now." I handed him another cold beer.

Taking a swig, he looked at me for a long moment. **You say some day we're going to be buddies? Buddies are important, they're not like civilian friends.**

"How do you mean?" I asked.

You share more with a buddy; your lives are in each other's hands every day. You're more like brothers. Civilian friends don't usually have that, they tell you not to do something

stupid when you're drunk. Buddies will post 360 security so you don't get caught.

Civilian friends call your parents Mr. and Mrs. But buddies call your parents Mom and Dad and wouldn't hesitate to tell them you were drunk as hell or about the fat chick you tried to pick up.[1]

Civilian friends hope the night out drinking goes smoothly, and hope that no one is late for the ride home. Buddies know some wild shit will happen, and set up rally points and an E & E route.[2]

A civilian friend will bail you out of jail and tell you what you did was wrong. Your Buddy will be sitting next to you saying, Damn...we screwed up...but hey, that crap was fun![3]

Civilian friends cry with you. Your buddies laugh at you and tell you 'Suck it up Cupcake.' Civilian friends borrow your stuff for a few days then give it back. You and your buddies steal each other's stuff so often nobody remembers who bought it in the first place.[4]

Civilian friends will listen to your relationship problems and hope it works out for you. Your buddy will listen to you over a long hard road march, and will help you straighten it out better than a Chaplin.[5]

Civilian friends know a few things about you. A Buddy could write a book with direct quotes from you.[6]

Civilian friends might try to hit on your girl behind your back, but your Buddy has spooned with you in foxholes more than your girl has, and would never even think about doing that.[7]

Civilian friends leave you behind if that's what the crowd is doing. A Buddy will kick the whole crowd's ass that left you. A civilian friend will knock on your door. A Buddy walks right in and says, 'I'm home!'[8]

Your civilian friends will try and talk to the bouncer when you get tossed out of the bar. A Buddy mans up and goes after the bouncer for touching you on the way out.[9]

Civilian friends will wish you had enough money to go out that night, and are sorry you couldn't come. Your buddies will share their last dollar with you, drag you along, and try to steal free drinks all night.[10]

There is only one bad thing about having buddies, he said sadly.

"What's that?"

Solemnly he said, *They die... right in front of your eyes.* He downed the last of the beer. *I really appreciate the beer. You say we'll meet again?*

"A few years from now."

He stood, picked up his helmet and set it on his head... chin strap dangling.

Till then, Buddy... got to get back to my unit. He shook my hand, saluted and slung the rifle over one shoulder and hurried off.

"Take care, Buddy," I said. "Be safe."

As he hit the brush again, he stopped, looked over one shoulder, waved and faded... along with the fog.

I waved back and whispered, "So long... Dad."

∞∞∞∞∞∞∞∞∞∞

*"...I want first of all—in fact, as
an end to these other desires
—to be at peace with myself.
I want a singleness of eye, a purity
of intention, a central core to my life
that will enable me to carry out these
obligations and activities as well as I can.
I want, in fact—to borrow from the language of the
saints—to live 'in grace' as much of the time as
possible. I am not using this term in a strictly theo-
logical sense. By grace I mean an inner harmony,
essentially spiritual, which can be translated into
outward harmony..."*[11]

41

Chapter Nine

Heroes aren't always heroic from our point of view. Johnny Mack Brown was an All-American halfback while attending the University of Alabama. He chose the silver screen over the green grass of the football field when he graduated. I thought he was a great cowboy and he was one of my heroes until I saw him at the County Fair.

He walked out on stage with his customary costume, a two-day beard and in an obvious state of what I believed to be inebriation.

He pulled his six-shooter, slurred his words and fired two shots into the heart of my hero worship.

In doing research for this book, another hero got painted in a completely different light. Iron Eyes Cody, the quintessential Native American—regal and stoic, one of the finest examples of the American Indian I ever saw. I was touched watching his epic commercial where one tear ran down his face because of mistreatment of the environment.

"Iron Eyes Cody portrayed Native Americans in Hollywood films and was actually born Espera Oscar de Corti. Cody was born April 3, 1904, in Kaplan, Vermillion Parish, Louisiana. He and his brothers moved to California as young men where they began acting in movies. At that time, they changed their surname to Cody. In 1996, his 100 percent Italian ancestry was confirmed by his half-sister."[1]

Neither man ever knew me, but both hurt me. One was never able to turn their fictional self into reality for themselves; the other was never able to turn their fictional self into reality for the world. One could not reconstruct the successes he had enjoyed when luck took him off the silver screen and made him a carnival attraction, and the other found fame being something he wasn't.

Heroes by their very nature are not common; nor are friends. As I learned the history of my heroes, I found they did not start out the way they ended up most of the time. I realized the same is true of friends.

Heroes BECAME what they were. I guess I have to let my friends do the same thing. Unfortunately, not everyone can be Roy Rogers or The Lone Ranger or Hopalong Cassidy. Damn shame... it is a gamble.

Pam shared this quote with me last night: "To love at all is to be vulnerable. Love anything and your heart will be wrung and possibly broken. If you want to make sure of keeping it intact you must give it to no one, not even an animal. Wrap it carefully round with hobbies and little luxuries; avoid all entanglements. Lock it up safe in the casket or coffin of your selfishness. But in that casket, safe, dark, motionless, airless, it will change. It will not be broken; it will become unbreakable, impenetrable, irredeemable... The only place outside Heaven where you can be perfectly safe from all the dangers of love... is Hell."[2]

∞∞∞∞∞∞∞∞∞∞∞∞

"I have had to experience so much stupidity, so many vices, so much error, so much nausea, disillusionment and sorrow, just in order to become a child again and begin anew. I had to experience despair, I had to sink to the greatest mental depths, to thoughts of suicide, in order to experience grace."[3]

Chapter Ten

Random thoughts and memories often jump into my mind; the trick is to figure out... WHY. One day in 1991, I was at a sports bar in Baton Rouge, Louisiana when my childhood hero Roy Rogers' picture was flashed on the television. Sadness gripped me, I knew he had died... A few days later, Paul Harvey commented that Roy was doing well after the heart attack and was expected to make a full recovery.

A couple of weeks after that, I received a Smoky Mountain Knife Catalog with Roy's picture on the front.

I felt I potentially had another chance to thank him for being one of my heroes growing up. I called Smoky Mountain and said, "This is Bob Anderson and I've lost Roy's phone number. Could you give it to me again?"

And they did! On November 21, 1991, I spoke to Roy Rogers on the phone... and he was exactly what he should have been.

"Roy Rogers—born Leonard Franklin Slye, November 5, 1911 – July 6, 1998, was an American singer and cowboy actor who was one of the most popular Western stars of his era. Known as the 'King of the Cowboys', he appeared in over 100 films and numerous radio and television episodes of *The Roy Rogers Show*. In many of his films and television episodes, he appeared with his wife Dale Evans, his golden palomino horse, Trigger, and his German Shepherd dog, Bullet.

"His show ran on radio for nine years before moving to television from 1951 through 1957. His productions usually featured a sidekick, often Pat Brady, Andy Devine or George 'Gabby' Hayes."[1]

He was much more than all of this, he was my hero. See for me "fictional" is not about stuff that is not real. It is about taking stuff that is not real and making it real, you could call this magic also.

If you are a reader, you can go places you'll never see. If you are a writer, you can take other people with you.

Think about it; me, a kid from Kilgore, Texas... I got to personally thank Roy for being there while I grew up and for being genuine. If that ain't magic... nothing is.

∞∞∞∞∞∞∞∞∞∞∞∞∞

> *"Gifts of grace come to all of us.*
> *But we must be ready to see*
> *and willing to receive these gifts.*
> *It will require a kind of sacrifice,*
> *the sacrifice of believing that,*

Grandfather Speaks Again

however painful our losses,
life can still be good—good in
a different way than before,
but nevertheless good. I will
never recover from my loss and
I will never get over missing the
ones I lost. But I still cherish life. . . .
I will always want the ones I lost
back again. I long for them with
all my soul. But I still celebrate the
life I have found because they are
gone. I have lost, but I have also
gained. I lost the world I loved,
but I gained a deeper awareness
of grace. That grace has enabled me
to clarify my purpose in life and
rediscover the wonder of
the present moment. "[2]

Chapter Eleven

A couple of days later, Pam had gone to town for groceries and I was working in my barn; really I was just piddling around. The weather was warmer; the sky was blue without a cloud anywhere. Yet, up my drive it looked like fog again. Since most of our neighbors are Amish, hoof beats coming down my driveway is not an unusual sound. However, a guitar being strummed is. I first noticed the rider was singing but I didn't immediately recognize the tune.

I'm a roaming cowboy riding all day long,
Tumbleweeds around me sing their
lonely song.
Nights underneath the prairie moon,
I ride along and sing this tune.[1]

I walked to the front of the barn and waiting. The next stanza I knew by heart and I sang out loudly and with force if not a lot of harmony:

See them tumbling down
Pledging their love to the ground
Lonely but free I'll be found

*Drifting along with the
tumbling tumbleweeds.*[2]

Through the dust and sunlight I watched him round the corner of my driveway. In the evening light I could see he was astride a big golden palomino. A pair of silver Colt .45s rode in a heavily-tooled, buscadero holster custom-fitted with sterling silver studs.

His double-creased, white Stetson sat back on his head. One leg was over the saddle horn. He reined in, *Howdy, mind if I step down?*

"Certainly not, I'm honored. Wrap the reins around the trailer over there," I said, trying to keep my surprise in check. "You were singing one of my favorite songs. I heard your boys down in Branson a couple of years ago. Wasn't the same without you, but they did real good. Out of respect, they had your hat sitting on the fence rail."

He smiled. *Friend of mine, fella named Bob Nolan, came up with it. Got famous in one of Gene's movies before me and the boys latched on to it. Guess we sort of took it over.* He smiled again, his blue eyes creasing, and changed the subject. *Could I trouble you for some water for my partner here?* he asked, petting the big horse's neck.

49

"Got a bucket right here," I said. "Would you... would you mind if I got it for him?"

Appreciate it... if it's not too much trouble.

"A privilege Sir, a privilege."

He stepped down, wrapped the reins and slung the guitar strap around the saddle horn. **Friend of ours suggested it would be alright if I stopped by. This a bad time?**

"Nope, couldn't be better. Does our friend wear buckskins?"

Yup.

I filled the bucket and walked to the palomino. His big eyes watched me approach and his nostrils flared trying to catch my scent. I held my hand out and the huge, soft, warm nose came into my hand. **He seems to like you,** the rider said.

"I like him too," I said, setting the bucket down. Rubbing his mane I said, "Hello big guy. It is a pleasure to finally meet you."

You know Smiley's the one that actually named him. When he saw him he said, 'that big horse is quick on the trigger'—it kind of stuck. He's fast and can stop on a dime and give you nine cents change.[3]

He can cut and spin so fast a lesser rider could be left in mid-air. Yet his personality is so good; I've put three or four kids on his back

at the same time and never worried they'd be hurt.[4]

With tears in my eyes, as I stroked the palomino, all I could say was, "He's magnificent." After a minute I said, "Smiley was one of your first sidekicks, right?"

He shook his head. ***Not one of... he was the first. He's a good guy; sidekicks are important people you know?***

I nodded, "So y'all are still in touch?"

Curiously, he said, ***Certainly, why wouldn't we be?***

I nodded. Rules of this world and life and death apparently did not work at this moment. "Yeah, sidekicks are important. I can't seem to find a good one though."

He looked at me sadly. ***You don't find them... They find you.***

"What do you mean? You had several; after all, who wouldn't want to be the sidekick for the King of the Cowboys?"

He smiled. ***You realize... I wasn't a cowboy in the beginning. Didn't become one until 1935. I wasn't born in Texas or Oklahoma or Arizona; born in Ohio. Son of a shoe maker, worked as a shoe maker myself, was a singer before I hit the trail in the movies.***[5]

51

"But it always seemed as though you and your sidekicks were really close."

He smiled again. Every time he smiled it was pure joy to watch. *We were, but remember we were actors. Gabby had never ridden a horse before the movies. He had to learn. George, his real self, was from New York, was a gourmet cook and a very intelligent fella.*[6]

Gabby was the character he became, and at that... he was the best that ever was. Each of my sidekicks was the best at what they did. They just did different things, different personalities, you see?[7]

"Maybe," I said. "So you didn't create them?"

Hahaha, he chuckled. *I could have never imagined them before I met them.* Then he looked at me seriously and said, *Could I?*

"Maybe that's my problem," I said. "I can see what people could be but they never are."

No, he said putting his hand on my shoulder. *You see what YOU think they could be, but they rarely are. Remember, they have a vote in what they are going to be... a bigger one than you have.*

That hung in the air for a while as it started to sink in; I think it started to sink in. But it would take some more thought to be sure and more conversation. None of which were apparently going to happen today. ***Thanks for the visit; I'll tell our friend I stopped by. Oh, and be easy with yourself. You will figure it out, I promise. See ya Pardner.***

"Come back anytime, I enjoyed it." He slung the guitar strap over his shoulder, grabbed the saddle horn with one hand and swung into the saddle.

Just like I'd seen him do a thousand times.

He wheeled the horse and slid the guitar around in one motion and headed back down the dirt driveway. The clip-clop of hooves, the strumming of the guitar and the last two stanzas faded into the evening and eventually gone, as he was... and that damned fog.

Cares of the past are behind
Nowhere to go but I'll find
Just where the trail will wind
Drifting along with the
tumbling tumbleweeds.
I know when night has gone
That a new world's born at dawn.
I'll keep rolling along
Deep in my heart is a song
Here on the range I belong

Bob Anderson

***Drifting along with the
tumbling tumbleweeds...***[8]

∞∞∞∞∞∞∞∞∞∞∞∞

*"All the natural movements of the soul are con-
trolled by laws analogous to those of physical
gravity. Grace is the only exception. Grace fills
empty spaces, but it can only enter where there is
a void to receive it, and it is grace itself which
makes this void. The imagination is continually at
work filling up all the fissures through which grace
might pass."*[9]

Chapter Twelve

Let me share something with you.

Magic is important in my family; Pixie Dust is also. Years ago our oldest granddaughter, Sarah, came for a visit with Pam and me, and we took her to the Renaissance Festival in Plantersville, Texas. It was as though we were transported back in time hundreds of years.

For two and a half hours, Pam and I had a great time watching Sarah experience the magic of being young and playing; but eventually Sarah tired out and was grumpy. As we were leaving, a beautiful winged Fairy stopped us, and with a purring voice, visited with Sarah who was absolutely enthralled.

The Fairy sprinkled Fairy Dust (or as I prefer to call it, Pixie Dust) on Sarah and she was good to go for another two hours. I learned that Pixie Dust (or glitter if you don't believe) is very powerful stuff, and as soon as we got back to Houston I went to the store to get some.

During the remainder of Sarah's visit, if she felt grumpy or behaved poorly, I'd bring out the Pixie Dust. Everything would change.

Why? Because she believed in the power of Pixie Dust. That belief gave her permission to behave differently than she felt. As she has grown up, her belief in the "validity" of Pixie Dust began to fall away.

That happens when bad things happen to good people. However, she continues to enjoy the magic of make believe because it makes her feel good. In fact, for her high school graduation, she got Pixie Dust from Pam and me.

There are enough things in each of our lives to make us feel bad. There is disease, death, taxes, war, abuse, neglect, debt, bankruptcy, divorce—all manner of things that slam into our world and send us spinning off into turmoil.

Sometimes, I think we need to remember that we each have it within us to take power from those things that slam into our world and send us spinning off into turmoil. But we have to believe in magic!

Last year Sarah stayed with us for two weeks, leaving us a wondrous gift—an Enchanted Forest. As a crow flies it is about fifty yards from my front door, along the walking path it is about 120 yards.

Nestled in a secluded part of our woods, along a gurgling spring, she had set up enchantment. A small metal patio table and two chairs painted gold, some Christmas decorations, and a couple of magic trolls guard the sanctuary. Years before Pam and I had created one for Sarah and Kayleigh, her sister, behind their home in a wooded lot.

Grandfather Speaks Again

When she first showed the Enchanted Forest to me, we talked about all things, big and small. It was a rough time for her and I was glad to see the old "magic" had not totally gone away. I told her how the Japanese may spend years "tuning" a spring so that as the water cascades over rocks, it makes a happy sound.

She moved a couple of rocks but didn't like the sound. I told her the secret to tuning a spring is being able to replace the rock in its original position if you don't like the sound, then move it again until the sound was what you wanted. Experimentation is necessary in life, as long as it's not permanent.

From time to time, I still visit the Enchanted Forest. That was where I saw him. I knew him, this wizard, we had met before.

Once, long ago, at a Renaissance Festival, I had felt a tap on my shoulder and turned. He was there, black robes with a tall peaked hat with wide brim. He handed me a wooden staff. I still have it. He said, **Here, you need this.** Had it not been for the reality of the staff, I would have called it a dream, a fantasy.

The morning was still, crisp... with the smell of cold. Fog was thick in the gully where the Enchanted Forest is. I turned the corner on the trail toward it and there he stood again.

I am...

"I know who you are. Am I dreaming? Are you a dream?"

A dream to some. A nightmare to others. I have walked my way since the beginning of time. Sometimes I give, sometimes I take, it is mine to know which and when![1]

"How did you get here?" I asked.

You brought me back. Your love brought me back. Back to where you are now. In the land of dreams. The days of my kind are numbered. The one God comes to drive out the many gods. [2]

The spirits of wood and stream grow silent. It's the way of things. Yes... it's a time for men, and their ways. My time is short with you, ask your questions.[3]

"Okay," I said breathlessly. "What is a lie? Must it be spoken or can action or inactions become a lie?"

When a man lies, he murders some part of the world; however, the lie manifests. It is evil of the worst kind, however it comes about.[4]

I was unnerved, almost scared by his words. "Where does evil hide in my world, then?"

Always... where you never expect it. Always. Remember, there's always something, someone, more clever than yourself. Good and evil, there never is one without the other. Once you have broken what could not be broken, hope is broken.[5]

"What does my future hold?"

Looking at the future is like looking at a cake. Until you've tasted it, what do you really know? And then, of course, it's too late. What are you afraid of? Shall I tell you what's out there?[6]

"Yes." Now fear was real in my heart.

He smiled. *The Dragon. A beast of such power that if you were to see it, whole and all complete in a single glance, it would burn you to cinders. It is everywhere! It is everything! Its scales glisten in the bark of trees, its roar is heard in the wind! And its forked tongue strikes like... like... lightening.*[7]

"Should I forgive, should I forget the wrongs done to me?"

You're not listening... well, your heart is not. Love is deaf as well as blind. For it is the doom of men that they forget. Look into the eyes of the dragon and despair!

Or not, the choice is yours. Do or do not do, act or do not act. Be or do not be, the choice is yours.[8]

"What then should I do?" I shouted, voice bordering on rage and fear.

Bob Anderson

Do nothing. Be still. Sleep. Rest in the arms of the Dragon. Dream.[9]

The fog grew thicker and he was gone.

∞∞∞∞∞∞∞∞∞∞∞∞

*"I hate and love. And why, perhaps you'll ask.
I don't know: but I feel tormented."*[10]

Chapter Thirteen

I tell people that I believe magic is the finger-print of God. Children are one example. It amazes me how the heart creates space as children come into your life. I remember how much love I felt when my son John was born; it filled me.

It didn't seem like there was any love left in the world. Then my daughter, Shelley, was born and I was filled up again. Totally... again.

But the real surprise was with my grandchildren. When my first granddaughter, Sarah, was born... filled up again.

Then a second granddaughter, Rachel... filled up again.

Then a third granddaughter, Kayleigh... filled up again.

Then a grandson, Josh... filled up again.

Then a second grandson, Seth... filled up again. How can a container be "filled up" again and again and again... without ever being emptied or the size of the container be increased?

That is the magic of the human heart.

The love I have for each is total... it was total on the first day of their lives. Yet, with each new one that love remained total... amazing isn't it?

Amazing because my love for each of them, and my appreciation of them as people, keeps growing.

Each is totally different and yet there are similarities. Each has courage, each has intelligence... each has their own magic. Each has taught me something.

Sarah—the magic of pixie dust. She is on the adventure of the "real world" and finding things aren't as simple as they looked from childhood. She's tougher now, yet on the inside... she still believes in Pixie Dust. In fact more now than a few years ago.

Rachel—being true to self. She is comfortable with who and what she is, a feminine, adventurous spirit—a sprite. As a child, she reminded me that we are all still children that like to play and see how far we can push the envelope of rules and boundaries; now she does it with grace and a kind spirit.

Kayleigh—an exuberant love of God and His creation. The joy and twinkle in her eye when speaking about the love she has for His Son—like an angel. Her courage, leadership, drive, vitality and enthusiasm are contagious to everyone she graces. I love this quote she sent us: "Every saint has a past, and every sinner has a future."

Joshua—pursing passion and drive. Working with his hands and his heart to create something he sees in his mind. His right of passage... moving from boy to man, he can see a vision of something in his mind because he has the magic of imagination. A powerful statement he shared in his last visit with Pam and Me: "Remember the past, focus on the present, dream of the future."

Seth—imagination and play. He is becoming more complex without becoming complicated. I treasure the long talks when he is here and the simple things. He is soulful, he is in balance between being tough or hard and too soft. His greatest quality right now.... a loyal spirit with a sense of right and wrong.

One thing each possesses is imagination. If they can imagine a better world, they can seek it, find it, or... knowing them—MAKE IT.

And each of them has courage and seeks that better world. Each gives me a hope for their future; and my own.

I love that as a grandparent, I can be more involved with my grandkids. It is not like when I was a kid and wasn't as involved with my grandparents. Mostly that was due to lack of technology and communication. In "the old days," we visited the grandparents but seldom talked on the phone.

Now the grandparents can visit the kids—see their world, meet their friends, walk in the dreamscapes they create.

My dad's father had died when he was a boy. I knew his mother, we all called her "Mom." She spent her time visiting each of her kids and bringing joy and love, and homemade apple pies, to each of us cousins.

Pappy and Nanny, my mother's parents, lived in the country and we visited them. I learned about the woods there, and things I keep finding in my memories as I get older. I don't know that a grandparent can ever be as active in their grandchildren's lives as they want to be. Nor do I know if they should be. It is a dance between being friendly and being a friend. My grandkids already have friends.

I treasure my role as PawPaw Bob. My role in their lives is to be me—something no one else can be. I don't want to be their best friend—I want to be their best PawPaw Bob. The grandparent role is something that you have to be in to understand.

As a grandparent, my goal is to make our home a safe place. Make it magic, make it real... make it a place they want to come to and are sorry to leave. But when they leave, they carry memories they will hold for a life time and, on occasion, when things are tough in their world... pull out and remember. I see that as my job.

I see a parent's job not to raise their children to be good people. I thought that way most of my adult life; I was wrong. My job was to raise my children well enough that they would raise their children to be good people. To let them grow, let them stumble. When they hurt... cry with them, sometimes for them, but let them grow. The parent's experience is important, but it is their world, their lives... theirs to live.

After all, we all made horrifying mistakes and survived. No one I know actually put out an eye with a Daisy Red Ryder BB Gun. We had no child-proof lids on medicine bottles, doors or cabinets and when we rode our bikes, we had no helmets, not to mention the risks we took hitchhiking.

As children, we would ride in cars with no seat belts or air bags. Riding in the back of a pick up on a warm day was always a special treat. We drank water from the garden hose and NOT from a bottle.

We shared one soft drink with four friends, from one bottle and no one actually died from this. We ate cupcakes, white bread and real butter and drank soda pop with sugar in it, but we weren't overweight because we were ALWAYS outside playing!

We would leave home in the morning and play all day, as long as we were back when the streetlights came on. No one was able to reach us all day. And we were okay. We would spend hours building our go-carts out of scraps and then ride down the hill, only to find out we forgot the brakes.

After running into the bushes a few times, we learned to solve the problem. We fell out of trees, got cut, broke bones and teeth and there were no lawsuits from these accidents. We ate worms and mud pies made from dirt, and the worms did not live in us forever.

We rode bikes or walked to a friend's house and knocked on the door or rang the bell, or just walked in and talked to them! Little League had tryouts and not everyone made the team. Those who didn't had to learn to deal with disappointment. Imagine that!

The idea of a parent bailing us out if we broke the law was unheard of. They actually sided with the law! Our generation produced some of the best risk-takers, problem solvers and inventors ever! We had freedom, failure, success and responsibility, and we learned how to deal with it all!

I tell my grandkids to "Live your life like it was a funny book." They have to believe in something. I want them to believe in God, believe in magic, believe in people, believe in heroes and believe that they will have some fun today—in spite of the world.

And to remember that when they believe, an angel gets their wings each time a bell rings, and fairies die if they don't believe in them, and all they have to do to fly is think happy thoughts, and most importantly of all—there's no place like home.

Their only real danger is in picking their friends.

∞∞∞∞∞∞∞∞∞∞

"Grace isn't a little prayer you chant before receiving a meal. It's a way to live." [1]

Chapter Fourteen

It was colder now and the snow crunched with each step as I made my way back to the Enchanted Forest two days later. I knew it was time to take another look at the table and decorations Sarah had left, and the bracing chill actually settled my mind.

The snow from the last two days, only about two inches, covered the ground, but wasn't difficult to walk through.

When I rounded the last corner in the path, I found a little area that had been protected somehow from winter's attempt to cover the ground.

The little stream still gurgled and the table and chairs were almost clean of snow. I wiped what was there off with my glove and sat down. The sun was boring through the trees and glistening off of each crystal of snow. The little stream danced with the pixie dust of its reflection on the water. It was quiet.

BUZZ, BUZZ! The sound was strange in this setting. With the cold, I hadn't expected dragon flies and wasps to be active.

BUZZ, BUZZ! I swatted at the sound behind my head. "Get outta here," I said, figuring it was an errant wasp not yet dormant.

BUZZ, BUZZ! ***Why should I leave?*** A small voice could be heard over the stream. ***This is my place, you know.***

I looked around but saw no one. Checking, I did not see any fog either...

You can choose to believe in something or nothing. You can choose to find magic in little things or turmoil in big things. It is your choice, make it![1]

I stood up and looked again. "Where are you?"

I'm here, right here. You're just not seeing.

Looking for a person standing on my property, I turned again, full circle.

You're looking for something big, I'm small... Look closer, I'm right here.

"I'll be damned," I said. "So you are." The sun caught the gossamer wings and danced. Five feet up, she stood on a twig—three inches tall. Blond hair with a tinge of amber, a leaf green outfit that looked like something from Robin Hood, complete with a little cap.

"Oh, my... you're a... are you a ...?"

Exasperated, she put both hands on her hip and turned her head. ***I am a... What do you think I am?***

"Are you a Fairy?"

Hallelujah, he understands!

"But... Fairies aren't..."

Watch it now, don't say that. You know what will happen if you say that.

"I know," I said quickly. "I'm sorry, it is just… you just surprised me."

Well, don't let your surprise be my downfall, please.

"Are you the only one? The only Fairy around here?"

Of course not Silly, there are a lot of us. You just never focus on little things like us, so you don't see us. We watch over you and Pam all the time. We come to the deck when you're having coffee, you hear us sometimes… but you don't see.

"I see," I said, but I didn't really.

No, you haven't. Not usually, you just don't have distractions right now. I had to wait until you could focus on the small.

"Well, you are small, beautiful but small."

She did a little pirouette on the twig. *Actually… thank you… Actually, I'm rather tall for Fairy folk.*

"Why did you decide to visit today?"

She cocked her little head to one side. *I didn't… you came to see me, remember?*

"I came to check the Enchanted Forest; I had no idea there were Fairies here."

Her wings buzzed furiously and both hands went back on her hips. ***Are you saying you don't believe in Fairies?***

"Heavens no." I knew how that would play out. "I do, I do believe in Fairies."

Good thing, we believe in you.

∞∞∞∞∞∞∞∞∞∞∞∞

"Grace is what picks me up and lifts my wings high above and I fly! Grace always conquers! Be graceful in everything; in anger, in sadness, in joy, in kindness, in unkindness, retain grace with you!"[2]

Chapter Fifteen

"Well, of course you would. I'm a real person."

Her wings buzzed angrily again. *And I'm...not...?*

"I didn't mean that the way it sounded," I cried. "Look, I've just never met any of you in person."

Sure you did, remember when you took Sarah to the Renaissance Festival? Remember when she first learned of Pixie Dust?

"Are you saying that Fairy was real?"

All Fairies are real, Silly. We come in all shapes and sizes. Remember how you felt when she talked to her. For a moment, you believed. You just have to believe. Didn't the Pixie Dust work on Sarah? Doesn't she still believe in its power?

Sadly, I said, "Probably not as much as then. She's older now, into the real world and the past has not always been gentle with her or my other grandchildren."

Your people are so fragile, not like Fairy folk. We grow up but sometimes... your people sometimes just grow old.

Some, the lucky ones, grow up without growing old—growing up is just a natural process of maturing.

Growing old means you lose the gift of play and the belief in magic. Those of your kind that grow up continue to see possibilities instead of obstacles.

You look for new ways to excel instead of settle. You learn that good guys don't always wear white hats and that bad guys don't always wear black.[1]

I smiled. "I have always said, 'Live your life like it was a funny book.' You have to believe in something, so I decided to believe in God and believe in magic."

And... Her head cocked menacingly again.

"Fairies of course. I believe in God and Fairies and magic."

Magic is His fingerprint, she said, quite pleased with herself, and flew off the twig to buzz around for a moment before lighting back on the twig. *That was fun.*

"So," I said a little stunned. "Fairies believe in God?"

Silly, how could we not?

∞∞∞∞∞∞∞∞∞∞∞∞

"Beauty without grace is like a fish far displaced from the water and looking at this kind of beauty is like watching that fish die right there on the cement in front of you."[2]

73

Chapter Sixteen

What else do you believe in? I wondered, before the words came to my lips. "What else do you believe in?"

All things worth having, nothing not worthy of being had. Fun and sometimes sadness, that depends on what is making us sad. And that is our choice. All things real, nothing unreal.

I smiled. "Well, nothing unreal exists."

Exactly, she buzzed. **Kiri-kin-tha's first law of metaphysics, nothing unreal exists.**

"You believe in Star Trek?" I asked stunned and amazed. "That was one of Mr. Spock's lines...?"

Fairies come in all shapes and fashions... but we all have pointed ears. Changing subjects, why have you been so sad of late?

"I don't know, things haven't gone exactly right. Sometimes it seems there is just too much drama in the world."

All drama has aspects of good and bad, beauty and ugliness, grace and turmoil. What determines the good, the beauty or the grace is your own attitude and willingness to 'own' your decision and make the best of it.

You are who you are not because of what happened to you, but because of how you chose to be and act after it happened.[1]

Remember the Fairy prayer, 'Don't cry because it is over, smile because it happened.'[2] *What else do you believe?*

"I know that what I want is within my power if... it only requires my effort. And if I want it bad enough. But everything involves more than it appears to. The easier it appears to be, the more there is that is hidden. Triumph does not come from the first attempt. Triumph comes AFTER overcoming the difficult and complex. Triumph arrives when 'What can be, becomes real.'"[3]

She nodded and said, sadly, *All dilemmas have aspects of good and bad, beauty and ugliness, grace and turmoil. Learning and improvement take place during the development of skills and abilities.*

This is called the 'doing' and it is difficult. The 'done' is when we have accomplished the task we set for our self. 'Done' is to be celebrated.[4]

A breeze came up and I could hear giggling floating on it. She turned her head, waved and said, *Got to run. See you soon. Oh, and remember, all of the world is made of faith, and trust, and pixie dust.*[5]

BUZZ BUZZ! She was gone.

I sat there realizing I never asked her name. Then I realized... I didn't have to ask.

∞∞∞∞∞∞∞∞∞∞∞

"Butterflies are self propelled flowers."[6]

Chapter Seventeen

As I turned to leave the Forest, the fog rolled in... I heard his footsteps first, then his voice. *Come sit with me. We will make talk, we will make smoke. There is much to learn.*

"Grandfather? You have never visited me during the day when I was awake," I said.

Really, I have never come to you in the daylight... and are you awake now? It is day and that makes our time together different? You white people...you see much, understand little and question everything.

"Did you see her?" I asked. "Did you see the Fairy?"

We do not call them that, that is a white word. She, like me, is just one of the 'people.' That is what we all call ourselves. Words have meaning, different meanings to different people. It is like energy.

Remember, there are all forms of positive and negative energy in the world. Trying to change another person to think, behave or be what we want of them creates negative energy, and it doesn't work.[1]

"I know," I said. "I can positively change my-self. That is positive energy, and that's the real source of happiness."

Exactly, it is the failures and bad things that have happened in your life that have made you who you are. We do not learn from success—we celebrate it. We learn best from failure and embarrassment. These are the things that have strengthened you and given you character and strength.

Why work diligently at something that when it's going as well as it possibly can, does not meet your needs? Why not spend that energy enjoying something that completes your soul and meets your needs. Don't do what feels good—do what makes you feel good as a person.[2]

There are differences in people, and the differences are usually pretty good. That is why society is made up of people, not a person. How boring to be all alike.

Every person has something to teach you. Some show you what to be and what to do. Others are just good examples of bad examples. We can learn from both. The world is full of joys and blessings that most folks don't see, but that is just because they aren't looking! What would you change in your life?[3]

"I've thought about that," I said. "What would I change if I could go back in time? What mistakes would I not make? What could I do to avoid hurting the people I have hurt? What disasters would I be able to avoid? But, I came to realize that all of the things I would like to change or avoid, or should have prevented, were part of what has made me who I am today."

Everything that has come into your life— every friend, every enemy, every opportunity, every failure, every accomplishment, every embarrassment, every goal achieved and every goal denied, have all worked together to make you exactly who you are at this moment. It is about what you believe.[4]

"So far, I believe you have sent friends to visit me." He smiled. "Will there be more?"

You have much to learn, and I think you are more receptive to some teachers than others. You are trying to make difficult decisions, remember this... It is not important what you decide—it is only important what you decide about what you decided.[5]

"Okay," I said. "What more do I have to learn?"

Real courage and real winning sometimes look like fear and losing. Courage is not the absence of fear. Courage is doing the right thing in spite of your fear. What is—is. There-fore, what is not—is not. And, it is what it is till it is not that anymore.

Usually it is you that has to change it. Get that—it is important![6]

Doing hard things requires courage and the ability to see past our own fears, failings and feelings. It is therefore for the greater good, not our comfort, that we must do hard things.[7]

Only spend your energy on people that want to be the best they can be. Everyone will tell you what they 'can do'; your job is to evaluate what they are 'doing'. These are some things you must learn, but there is one more important than all the rest.[8]

"And what pray tell... what would that be?" I asked, genuinely curious.

Sometimes, there is no answer to a question. You just have to live through it.

∞∞∞∞∞∞∞∞∞∞∞∞

"Life makes fools of all of us sooner or later. But keep your sense of humor and you'll at least be able to take your humiliations with some measure of grace. In the end, you know, it's our own expectations that crush us."[9]

Chapter Eighteen

The howling started off in the distance and Grandfather started to fade, his last words, **You still have much to learn, my son. And much to remember.**

Since we live in a rural area, dogs howling are a fairly common event. Sometimes, late in the evening or early in the morning, the coyotes sing. Sometimes, a lone one sings trying to find companions; or maybe just sending a prayer up to the moon. Sometimes, families can be heard, little yaps from the pups and long songs sung by their parents.

Hunting dogs after possums and raccoons often join in. Sometimes our neighbor's dogs will sound off because wildlife is moving through the morning mist or the still evening. Deer and turkeys, lions and tigers and bears, oh my!

Often, a long howl erupts from my pasture where my Red Tick Hound, Taffy, is on the hunt for a mole. That howl I have learned. A long AHOOOO will sound and I'll look up to see her tail straight up in the air and her head buried to her shoulders in a hole she has dug.

Taffy is a rescue dog; saved by my grandkids... she is deaf from beatings she received in Louisiana. They decided "Pawpaw Bob needs another dog." No hearing in her ears, but a great nose and good eyes. Often she will set off in song threatening whatever wildlife has dared to patrol HER forty acres.

The sounds of running paws and crashing brush were getting closer. They were coming out of the fog and straight down the hill through the brush; right at me. I could barely see the lead dog, a big black... maybe a Labrador. He stopped thirty yards from me and waited for the rest of the pack. He was followed by the most motley crew of dogs I had ever seen run together. A small white, looked like a Poodle... had twigs hanging from her ears and tail. Followed by a bundle of red and tan; slightly bigger in size. Following the others came a grey, black, tan and white Australian Shepard with one blue eye.

Grandfathers words came to me again. ***My son, all animals speak. It is man's responsibility to hear. In the old days, we spoke the same language. That was before man changed. Some of us still listen and can hear.***

The big black sat on his haunches; his thick, heavy tail thumping the ground. ***Hi, Dad,*** he said as clear a day.

Grandfather Speaks Again

∞∞∞∞∞∞∞∞∞∞

"Love is holy because it is
like grace—the worthiness of its object
is never really what matters."[1]

Chapter Nineteen

"Jack, Jack Daniels... is it you?" I cried.

Yeah, it's me and the rest of the guys. We needed to talk to you. Jack was a Lab and Rhodesian Ridgeback mix I found as a puppy, just eight weeks old. He lived with us for fourteen years.

Hi Dad, Muffin, the little white Poodle and Lhasa mix said as she bounded over to me. Her coat was cut short except for her ears and tail, she was quite lovely. **Love me, love me. It has been so long.**

I sat down and she leaped in my lap, licking my face and trying to scrim closer to me. I had found her wet and abandoned on the side of the rode; she stayed with us sixteen years. Carefully I removed the twigs she had picked up with those soft ears and flashing tail.

The Aussie had his head down low and watched me with his eyes, looking like a coyote on the prowl... as usual. "Gib, Gibson? You're here!"

Missed you Dad, how's Mom?

"She misses you Gib. It broke her heart that she wasn't here when you left." I looked around at the rest of them. "It hurt her when each of you left."

Gib almost smiled, *I'm glad she wasn't here, Dad. You know how she is, that would not have been good for her. It was better the way it happened.*

Yeah, Jack said. *I feel the same way, it would have hurt her. I remember how it was with Buddha.*

Muffin stopped squirming and sat primly. *Me too,* she said. *She has such a gentle heart; I didn't want her to see me like that. I still come to visit her, when she is sleeping.*

The red and tan, His Highness, Buddha the Great, had stayed back letting the others have their turn. Part Pekinese and part Pomeranian, he looked like a Chinese Temple Dog; ergo the name. One of love, not disrespect. Like the first Buddha, he taught us peace and love, mostly love. Finally, regally, he came forward. *How are you, Dad?*

"I'm in shock Buddha, how are you?"

I'm always good, you know that. By the way, thanks for bringing me with you and Mom. I love this place; I never, ever had so much room to run.

"We could not leave you in Texas when we came here, even though you were... You know. We wanted you with us."

I'm glad but I know it was hard for you and Mom.

I nodded. "One of the hardest things we ever did. But... it was worth it to have you with us. Can you... can you come with me and let Mom have a visit?"

Buddha sat next to me and licked Muffin's eyes. ***Nope. We can't do that, it would not be right. It would upset her. It is better we keep visiting with her the way we do. It is better when she is sleeping, easier for her to deal with us in the dream world.***

I nodded. "You know you taught me and Mom a lot."

I did? What?

"You taught us love and grace more than anything else. You were... consistent I guess. You were always you."

Who else would I be?

"People aren't like dogs, Buddha. They don't always tell the truth."

Maybe they don't know what the truth is?

"Maybe." I thought about that. "I don't know. I do know that you and Muffin taught us a lot about love. Mom still talks about writing, *The World According to Buddha and Muffin.*"

I had never heard a dog laugh before, but I did at that moment.

We tried to come back to you, I tried to train Gibson.

86

"He was a lot like you... Thanks for doing that. Gib reminded us so much of you. When we got Annie, she didn't know much, remember?

Gibson said, **She didn't know how to eat from a bowl, only wanted to tear the bag to get to her food. She had lived on the street as a stray for so long. Now, she's like Muffin. Muffin's personality but bigger.**

Buddha said, **Can you say DEMANDING?**

It was my turn to laugh. Gibson nudged closer. **So... What's going on with you. Grandfather said you were not happy?**

"You know Grandfather?"

Of course, why do you think we're here?

"I... I don't know. But I'm awfully glad you guys came."

Muffin said, **Talk, talk, talk, I want to play. I want a game.**

I stood up. "A game it is. Which one?"

Chase! Catch me if you can! And the game was on. We ran in circles, around trees, through the stream, over rocks. I chased them, they chased me. On and on and on... Buddha ran, Muffin chased him, Jack focused on me and we ran back and forth. Me chasing him, him chasing me. I chased them all. Gib watched.

Bob Anderson

"Dogs are our link to paradise. They don't know evil or jealousy or discontent. To sit with a dog on a hillside on a glorious afternoon is to be back in Eden, where doing nothing was not boring—it was peace."[1]

Chapter Twenty

Finally, I was out of breath and sat down. Gibson came over and laid his head in my lap and closed his eyes as I scratched his head. The others kept the game going. "I'm sorry I could not save you Gib."

It was time, I was sick. You did what you could... You loved me.

"I still do. I think of you all of the time."

We like Annie and Taffy, Taffy is so funny with the moles. Annie is still as bossy as ever.

I laughed. "She is that."

I come to see her sometimes and we play. I love her. I loved Muffin too, she was my first love. But it was always her and Buddha; I just filled in for him.

The other dogs kept running, twisting, turning and playing. I sat there a long time, rubbing Gibson and watching them. It was peaceful, a peace I hadn't felt in a long time. It's funny how you don't realize how bad your hurt... until the pain is taken away.

Jack stopped running and walked to me. His huge tongue left my cheek wet with dog spit. *Dad... I think it is time for us to go.* Gibson sat up.

"I wish you would stay."

Buddha came over. **We'll be back. You know we're never really far away.**

"I don't want you to leave. It's the first time we've talked."

You talk about us and to us all the time, we can hear you. We talk to you all the time; this is just the first time you've heard us. We'll be back. Remember; we're never really far away. You can talk to us any time.

Muffin climbed back in my lap. **I want loving.** I hugged her as hard as I could.

"Take care of them, Muffin, you are still the boss dog."

She smiled. **I know. They are such... boys. I'll watch them. Tell Mom...**

"I will," I said. "She loves you too."

Jack stopped in his tracks, I knew that look. It was the one he used to get before he would run away and get in trouble with the Houston Puppy Police, as I called them. He looked at me then he looked at the woods and back at me. "Go ahead Jack, have fun." He was off, Muffin chasing, barking insistently at his heels.

Buddha turned. **You're okay now, aren't you?** I nodded. **You know, it is all about love. You loved us, we love you. One of your people** *said, Love is all you need. He was right, you know.* He ran after the others.

Gibson was the last to leave. *Are you okay?* he asked, ever the gentleman, ever the loving one. Who says a dog can't be thoughtful. No demands, just love. Anything that can dream, that can love, has to have a soul. Gibson is the best example. Unconditional love, ever the protector, ever the gentleman.

I nodded. "Be safe Gib, watch out for them."

Don't I always? Even Muffin needs watching. I'll keep them herded and safe. His head dropped, that coyote look was back. *I'll watch over you and Mom,* he said, and was gone. The barking faded into nothingness and the world was still again.

∞∞∞∞∞∞∞∞∞∞

"When grace moves in... guilt moves out"[1]

Chapter Twenty-One

The dogs came back to show me that with as many mistakes I had made with each of them, I had done my best to honor the thoughts written below. I saw this on our Veterinarian's wall a long time ago:

Treat me kindly, my beloved master, for no heart in all the world is more grateful for kindness than the loving heart of me.

Do not break my spirit with a stick, for though I should lick your hand between the blows, your patience and understanding will more quickly teach me the things you would have me do.

Speak to me often, for your voice is the world's sweetest music, as you must know by the fierce wagging of my tail when your footstep falls upon my waiting ear.

When it is cold and wet, please take me inside... for I am now a domesticated animal, no longer used to bitter elements... and I ask no greater glory than the privilege of sitting at your feet beside the hearth... though had you no home, I would rather follow you through ice and snow than rest upon the soft-est pillow in the warmest home in all the land... for you are my god... and I am your devoted worshiper.

Keep my pan filled with fresh water, for although I should not reproach you were it dry, I cannot tell you when I suffer thirst. Feed me clean food, that I may stay well, to romp and play and do your bidding, to walk by your side, and stand ready, willing and able to protect you with my life, should your life be in danger.

And, beloved master, should the Great Master see fit to deprive me of my health or sight, do not turn me away from you. Rather hold me gently in your arms as skilled hands grant me the merciful boon of eternal rest...and I will leave you knowing with the last breath I drew, my fate was ever safest in your hands.[1]

The dogs helped me realize I was okay, I was a good person. Maybe not the best person, I could improve. But after all, my dogs... my four legged friends knew me for the person I was and loved me anyway. "I think we are drawn to dogs because they are the uninhibited creatures we might be if we weren't certain we knew better. They fight for honor at the first challenge, make love with no moral restraint, and they do not for all their marvelous instincts appear to know about death. Being such wonderfully uncomplicated beings, they need us to do their worrying."[2]

I've heard it said, "The way to have a good life was to try to be the kind of person your dog already thinks you are."[3] Also, "You should not take your dog's affection as conclusive evidence you're a nice person."[4]

I would work at being as good as they thought I was... think I am, evidently. Frankly, however, I doubted it would work as well on people as it did with pups.

I like dogs better than I do most people. Did you ever notice dog is God spelled backward?

Pam and I "inherited" Taffy from our grandkids. Fate arranged for them to come together. Beaten so badly that she is deaf, she can't hear anything. Good news is she is "dog" sociable. Most of her training was done by, and revolved around, Gibson and Annie. She learned to trust us. Since she is smart, she's been able to learn hand signals. Gib and Annie became her ears, and Taffy let Pam and me find a place in her heart.

I've heard many good quotes about dogs:

"If there ain't dogs in heaven, I'll go to where they are!"[5]

"The reason a dog is such a comfort when you're blue is they are smart enough not to try and figure out why you are blue."[6]

"The average dog is nicer than the average person."[7]

"If you pick up a starving dog and make him prosperous, he will never bite you; that is the main difference between dogs and people."[8]

"Dogs love their friends and bite their enemies, quite unlike people..."[9] I can't agree more!

"If I have any thoughts about immortality it is that certain dogs I have known will go to heaven and very few people."[10] Amen.

My issue was not with dogs, it was with people. There are reasons I like dogs and other critters better than most people. Dogs and critters... they don't lie to you. They don't lie about you. They don't steal from you. They don't cheat. I saw a report the other day that said dogs even understand fair. So as you're passing out treats remember they can't count, but they understand being fair. I'm not sure I agree that they can't count; put three dog biscuits in our pocket and see what happens when you just give out two.

∞∞∞∞∞∞∞∞∞∞∞

"A family in my sister's neighborhood was recently stricken with a double tragedy, when both the young mother and her three-year-old son were diagnosed with cancer. When Catherine told me about this, I could only say, shocked, 'Dear God, that family needs grace.' She replied firmly, 'That family needs casseroles,' and proceeded to organize the entire neighborhood into bringing that family dinner, in shifts, every single night, for an entire year. I do not know if my sister fully recognizes that this IS grace."[11]

Chapter Twenty-Two

A day or so later, I was walking down the drive-way to the mail box and had just rounded the curve in my driveway and started down the incline when I stopped. A gentleman on a large buckskin had dismounted his horse and was waiting for me. *Didn't think you'd be so late.*

"Wasn't aware I had a place to be," I said. He wore a derby hat and was leaning on a black walk-ing stick with a gold knob. The vest, dress shirt and tie, coupled with a nickel plated six gun in a cross draw holster under his dress western coat, told me who he was. "Pleasure to meet you Mr. Mas..." He held up a finger to stop me.

Friends call me Bat. I understand you are a writer also. I'm a sports writer, editor, and a columnist for a paper in New York City. I understand you also had a background in law enforcement, like me.

I nodded. "Not as heralded as yours but I did okay."

He laughed. *Most of that heraldry was total hog wash. Got started off as a practical joke. A friend of mine, Dr. W.S. Cockrell, fed a big line to a reporter looking for a story one time in Gunnison, Colorado. The reporter asked Dr.*

W.S. Cockrell about man killers and Doc pointed at me and said, 'That's Bat and he's killed 26 men.'[1]

Cockrell kept the reporter's attention with several lurid tales about my 'exploits' and the fool wrote them up for the New York Sun. Soon the stories were widely reprinted in papers all over the country and became the basis for many more exaggerated stories told about me over the years.[2] *But that is secondary to our visit; how can I help you?*

"What do you know about friendship?"

Whoa, that's a heavy topic, friend. You sure you want to go there?

"Just looking for some input, I won't hold you to it."

Friends come in all sizes, shapes and complexions. You can have casual friends who happen to share interests, attitudes and ideas that resemble your own. They may even be just around the corner from you, that helps in friendships. They can be comfortable, reliable... until things get difficult.

You can have some that are in your life more by circumstance than desire. They are 'friendly' and there isn't anything really 'wrong' with them; things just never develop any further than surface stuff.

Shucks, from what I have seen of your world today… with all of this socializing media, texting, email, instagram, or whatever comes out next, your folks are having intimate relationships with folks that you have never met and probably won't ever meet. It all makes the hair on the back of my head stand straight up.

He reached into his inside coat pocket and pulled out a piece of paper. He unfolded it and handed it to me. *Here are some thoughts about friendships that you might want to use to evaluate what passes for friendships in your world.* It read…

~A true friend is someone who thinks that you are a good egg even though he knows that you are slightly cracked.[3]

~A friend is one who knows us, but loves us anyway.[4]

~Remember, the greatest gift is not found in a store nor under a tree, but in the hearts of true friends.[5]

~Your friend is the man who knows all about you, and still likes you.[6]

~What is a friend? A single soul dwelling in two bodies.[7]

~*The best way to destroy an enemy is to make him a friend.*[8]

~*Some people come into our lives and quickly go. Some stay for awhile and leave footprints on our hearts. And we are never, ever the same.*[9]

~*One who looks for a friend without faults will have none.*[10]

~*A real friend is one who walks in when the rest of the world walks out.*[11]

~*A friend hears the song in my heart and sings it to me when my memory fails.*[12]

~*A companion loves some agreeable qualities which a man may possess, but a friend loves the man himself.*[13]

~*Friends show their love in times of trouble...*[14]

~*My friend is he who will tell me my faults in private.*[15]

~*We cannot tell the precise moment when friendship is formed. As in filling a vessel drop by drop, there is at last a drop which makes it run over; so in a series of kindnesses there is at last one which makes the heart run over.*[16]

~*It's the ones you can call up at 4:00 a.m. that really matter.*[17]

~*A true friend is someone who is there for you when he'd rather be anywhere else.*[18]

I read them quickly and nodded as I folded the paper and stuck it in my back pocket. "You know, often in the military, friends don't speak for months or years, but when they talk again... it seems the conversations start where they left off so long ago and the friendship is kick started without interruption."

The term 'friendship' gets thrown around a lot... even to people you don't even know and will never meet. But that doesn't mean these people are truly your friends. I've heard it said 'the best friendships have an in-depth relationship combining trust, support, communication, loyalty, understanding, empathy, and intimacy. You must be able to trust and relax with your friend; that is a big part of friendship. The feeling of—I'm home, I can relax now.[19]

"No one can form a friendship until he or she realizes that the basis of being friends is meeting the needs of the other person. I think the only way to have a friend... is to be one."[20]

Maybe so, but a good friendship is like a good story; it doesn't have to be true... it just has to be good. Several times, I sold my famous six gun because I 'needed the money.' Most of the time, I'd buy old guns at pawnshops, carve notches into the handles and sell

them at inflated prices. Each time I claimed the gun was the one I used during my career as a lawman. Not true but it was a good story.[21] He smiled.

He slid the cane into loops on the saddle and mounted the buckskin. **Hope that helps you**. He doffed his derby hat and swung the buckskin around and galloped off down the drive singing, **Back when the west was very young, there lived a man named...**[22] before fading away.

There was no fog this time when the visitor came.

∞∞∞∞∞∞∞∞∞∞∞∞

"Fiction is obliged to stick to possibilities.
Truth isn't."[23]

Chapter Twenty-Three

It was the next day before Grandfather returned. I asked him, "Grandfather, why have our peoples always been at war with each other? Even now, you are not treated fairly."

It was not always so, in the beginning it was different. In the beginning, we were neighbors. We even helped create one of your holidays. Tisquantum of the Pawtuxet tribe, your people knew him as Squanto, taught the Pilgrims about the land, where to hunt, and how to plant corn. Tisquantum had been captured by your people in 1605 and taken to England where he learned your language.[1]

One of your people...

"Captain John Smith?"

Yes, Captain Smith brought him back to New England. Before that, your people wanted to have a feast to give thanks. They provided deer, turkey, water birds and fish, plus what they had harvested: wheat, corn and barley. My people brought clams, mussels, lobster, eel, ground nuts, acorns, black walnuts, chestnuts, squashes, and beans, along with fruits and berries such as strawberries, raspberries, grapes, and gooseberries that were growing

wild. It seemed for a while our peoples could live in peace and brotherhood.[2]

"But, as John Greenleaf Whitter once said, '*For of all sad words of tongue or pen, the saddest are these—it might have been!*'"

Yes, he said sadly, **It might have been, but it was not to be. But we held the belief that it would be. In fact, we still do.**

[**belief, a noun. plural noun: beliefs.** An acceptance that a statement is true or that something exists. Something one accepts as true or real; a firmly held opinion or conviction. opinion, view, conviction, judgment, thinking, way of thinking, idea, impression, theory, conclusion, notion, trust, faith, or confidence in someone or something. Faith, trust, reliance, confidence.][3]

I said, "My people believed we had a manifest destiny to occupy the entire continent."

What is this manifest thing you speak of?

"A right and obligation to us by God. We believed the expansion of the U.S. throughout the American continents was both justified and inevitable."

[**believe, a verb, present: believes; past tense: believed.** Accept something as true; feel sure of the truth of. Be convinced by, trust, have confidence in, consider honest, consider truthful, regard as true, accept, be convinced by, give credence to, credit, trust, put confidence in; accepting the statement of someone as true. Have faith, especially religious faith. Feel sure that someone is capable of a particular action.][4]

You had no right to take that which you do not own. My people knew we could not sell Mother Earth; it was not ours to sell. Neither, my son, was it your people's right to take that which did not belong to you. It was not justified but it was inevitable.

We greeted you as brothers, your people killed mine, took our land... That one is capable of an action does not mean that the action is right.

Now, you hold all of the land from shore to shore. Land that was not yours, all of the land, except those parcels your government assigned to us. That is what your manifest thing was, nothing more.

Now, my people live on reservations or must appear as white men to survive.

Manifest...buffalo dung!

∞∞∞∞∞∞∞∞∞∞∞

"Our age not only does not have a very sharp eye for the almost imperceptible intrusions of grace, it no longer has much feeling for the nature of the violences which precede and follow them."[5]

Chapter Twenty-Four

The next morning, I sat in the open bay of my barn, thinking... *People, why do people and ghosts have to behave like... People?* The sound of hoof beats came again and I looked up. A man in black, riding a big black stallion was cantering up.

Good afternoon, Sir, he said in a cultured, baritone voice that hinted of steel. The dust from the trail had streaked his outfit. He kicked his small brim Stetson back on his head, dark curls spilling out.

"Good afternoon," I said. "Would you like to step down?"

I appreciate that, he said, and climbed down from the big black. The sun glinted off the sterling silver chess piece on his low-slung black leather holster. **It's a hot day,** he said.

"Would you care for a drink of water?"

He smiled; a thin dark mustache marked his upper lip. **Water would do if you don't have anything stronger.**

"Whiskey?" I asked. He nodded. "Step inside, take a chair," I pointed. He removed his hat and slapped it on his leg sending up a small cloud of dust; several other slaps cleared his clothes. I looked outside again to be sure... no fog.

I understand you may have need of me, he said, pulling a business card from beneath his gun belt.

Holy crap, I thought, the address was San Francisco. I had seen this card on hundreds of episodes. "So, you are real?"

As real as you, he said as he reached down and pulled a thin, dark cigar from the top of his boot. *Mind if I smoke?*

I poured two shots of whiskey. "Not at all, I'll join you." I pulled a cigar from my pocket and rolled the striker wheel on my Zippo, offering him a light first. "Looks like you've been on the trail for a while."

He nodded. *It's a long way from San Francisco. How may I be of assistance?*

I thought for a long moment, the whiskey warming my gut. "Trying to make some decisions about people and life."

He frowned. *A man can be hired to do anything in this world for another man but make a decision for him!*[1]

"Well, I wasn't exactly figuring on hiring you. I would like some perspective if you don't mind. I may stumble in my asking, the topic is a little scary to me."

Fire away, I sometimes think that all good men are afraid. It's also been said that fear is the beginning of wisdom.[2] *Who are you having trouble with?*

"My friends," I said, with a smile that did not convey humor.

He interrupted. *Some friendships are like a good wine; a wise man lets them age before sampling.*[3]

Sam Clemens once said, 'An enemy can partly ruin a man, but it takes a good-natured, injudicious friend to complete the thing and make it perfect.'

"My last one, my last friend... I don't feel re-spected me."

Respect is important to all men. Some will even risk death for it. It can be as contagious as measles if it's properly spread around.[4]

"I don't know if I am brave enough to gamble again on hurt feelings."

I have found no book on bravery, no formula for courage. I think perhaps a man is valiant only when his fear of cowardice exceeds his fear of death.[5] His hand flashed down and jerked the dark .45 free of the holster. *With this gun, I stopped murder. In all my life I've only seen a dozen real killers, but I've seen ten thousand people that would stand by and let it happen. Which is the greater evil?*[6]

I smiled, seeing the weapon in real life and not just in colors of black and white from the television. It was well oiled, well used but appeared like it was new. "You've come to offer me some lessons I presume. Now you are a teacher as well?"

He nodded. ***Without teachers, every generation would have to start by discovering fire and inventing the wheel. Which lessons are you in most need of?***[7]

I thought, *This is not a man you give a glib answer to.* I took a pull on the whiskey and a deep draw on the cigar. I said, "Tell me about life and betrayal. You have seen some of both I know."

My friend Gabby says, 'Life is tough and then you die.' Life can't be avoided, if you are going to live, betrayal is part of it. Betrayal causes trouble and trouble cannot be avoided, it will hunt you out. You must be willing to stand your ground. Otherwise, go home. Go home to your castle and lock the door and practice 'dip the knee' to your princely heart's content.[8]

But you can't stay there. Don't stay there unless you're prepared to sacrifice your illusions, and possibly even your life. You must be willing to stand against ignorance and prejudice. Ignorant and prejudiced people like to be

deceived; they don't like being confused with the truth?[9]

"Gabby is right," I said. "Life is hard, being a friend is even harder."

You have not reached the end of your trail yet; the good die young so they may not be corrupted, and the wicked live on so they may have a chance to repent. Are you still trying to repent?[10]

"I don't know about repenting, I think I'm working on some redemption," I said, wondering about the distinction I was making.

His eyes grew hard. *Repenting, redemption, sometimes the difference is only in our superstitions. Sometimes I feel very superior to a Chinese friend of mine. I forget that he comes by his superstitions honestly; he learned them from the cradle.* He stared at me hard for a moment, *You don't have that excuse, do you?*

"No," I said. "I have studied, I have searched. The answers just keep escaping me."

Maybe you are looking too hard. Often it is like wine, some good wines are better slightly chilled.[11]

"How do you choose a friend?"

He thought for a long moment. *I met Oscar Wilde once, he told me, 'I choose my friends for their good looks, my acquaintances for their good characters, and my enemies for their intellects. A man cannot be too careful in the choice of his enemies.'*

"How do you deal with a friend that doesn't tell you the truth?"

Oscar also said, 'Man is least himself when he talks in his own person. Give him a mask, and he will tell you the truth.'

I shook my head in frustration. "But I'm a writer; I want to leave important words that will be remembered. I want to help people with the struggles I have had."

Do you write literature for the ages or journalism for the newspapers?

"I have done both but now I write novels."

Wilde said, 'The difference between literature and journalism is that journalism is unreadable and literature is not read.'

"My struggle, this friendship thing, seems to take forever."

Impatience is not a bad thing when controlled. And mercy is often better than revenge. Oscar told one of his friends, 'If you are not too long, I will wait here for you all my life.'

He also reminded me, 'The only difference between the saint and the sinner is that every

saint has a past, and every sinner has a future.'

"I just want things to work out; I'm tired of all
the drama. I'm tired of feeling used and underap-
preciated. Why does doing good meet so much re-
sistance?"

He laughed a booming laugh. **Heaven help us,
what men do in the name of good.**[12] **Good luck,
a man benefits from a worthy quest. Enjoy
yours... at least benefit from it.**

He reset his Stetson, climbed onto the big black
still smoking the cigar. Before he was half way
down my driveway... he and the big black horse
faded from view. All that was left was the two
empty whiskey glasses and the smell of cigar
smoke... and the business card in my hand.

∞∞∞∞∞∞∞∞∞∞∞

*"You must pay for everything in this world one
way and another. There is nothing free except the
Grace of God. You cannot earn that
or deserve it."*[13]

Chapter Twenty-Five

I'm trying to explain that trust and respect are important to me and I didn't feel my "friends" had respected me, so I didn't trust them. I am not the only one to have this happen, others have pondered the issue. I've heard a few powerful sayings in this regard:

"People that have trust issues only need to look in the mirror. There they will meet the one person that will betray them the most."[1]

"There is no respect between the souls of two individuals if their minds can't trust each other and there is no trust between them if their hearts can't accept the truth of each other."[2]

"I'm not concerned with your liking or disliking me. All I ask is that you respect me as a human being."[3]

"Respect begins with this attitude: 'I acknowledge that you are a creature of extreme worth. God has endowed you with certain abilities and emotions. Therefore I respect you as a person. I will not desecrate your worth by making critical remarks about your intellect, your judgment or your logic. I will seek to understand you and grant you the freedom to think differently from the way I think and to experience emotions that I may not experience.' Respect means that you give the other person the freedom to be an individual."[4]

For me, what you say is not as important to me as what you do, as exampled by this saying: "Some of the most unkind, judgmental people I've ever known go to church every Sunday and read the Bible. I don't know how some people are able to disassociate their own cruelty and shortcomings from their religious obligations and convictions, but many are able to do that."[5]

"If a person loves you but doesn't respect you then it cannot be a real love. It is not possible to love them without respecting them."[6]

My definition of a friend is simple: A person with whom I have a relationship with, and our interactions guided by respect, trust and goodwill. A person I enjoy spending time with, either face-to-face or via phone. A person with whom I can share dreams, goals, challenges, struggles… pretty much anything with, and know that I can trust them with that part of me, have my back—and vice versa. A person that will have courage to be honest and straight with me if it looks like I'm believing my own B.S, if I'm out of line, or doing something that would hurt our friendship—and vice versa.

I also feel my rules for friendship are simple:

- If you wish to be my friend… be there when you say you will be, as I am.
- Do what you said you will do, as I do. If something changes that keeps you from being there or doing what you have said, call me and tell me… as I will do for you. I do not wish to change you but I do believe you and I can improve each other with honesty, respect and accountability.
- The biggest part of being my friend involves trust and respect.
- I decided you were my friend because you are who you are. However, if I can no longer trust you or you no long trust me, why are we spending time together?

- Some things are simply non-negotiable. If I make an agreement with you and circumstances beyond my control keep me from honoring it, I will tell you and I won't wait until the last minute. That might create a problem for you.

- If you make an agreement with me and circumstances beyond your control keep you from honoring it; I expect... No, I require the same consideration. UNLESS a new agreement has been made... the old agreement remains in effect. I will hold up my end and expect you to do the same.

- Do not ignore me, do not disrespect me... those are not the actions of a friend. Respect is a reciprocal commodity. I will not ignore you, unless you ignore me.

I have felt rage, sought revenge. Felt guilt and sought grace and redemption.

I still believe there are times when anger is a positive emotion, when a person should "draw a line in the sand" and say, NO MORE! Some people need boundaries to protect themselves. Other people need to be kept within boundaries to keep from hurting others. So true, so sad!

∞∞∞∞∞∞∞∞∞∞

"It is peace not war that destroys men; it is comfort not danger that breeds cowardice. It is plenty, not need that breed greed and avarice."[7]

"Friendship is always a sweet responsibility, never an opportunity."[8]

"Friendship is born at that moment when one person says to another: 'What! You too? I thought I was the only one.'"[9]

"An insincere and evil friend is more to be feared than a wild beast; a wild beast may wound your body, but an evil friend will wound your mind."[10]

"I value the friend who for me finds time on his calendar, but I cherish the friend who for me does not consult his calendar."[11]

"Growing apart doesn't change the fact that for a long time we grew side by side; our roots will always be tangled. I'm glad for that."[12]

Grandfather Speaks Again

"Friends are the family you choose."[13]

"Every friendship travels at some time through the black valley of despair. This tests every aspect of your affection. You lose the attraction and the magic. Your sense of each other darkens and your presence is sore. If you can come through this time, it can purify with your love, and falsity and need will fall away.
It will bring you onto new ground where affection can grow again."[14]

Chapter Twenty-Six

My next visitor came up my drive a day later. He was a small, almost emaciated little brown man with wire frame glasses and a grey mustache. His arms, barely larger than the wooden staff he carried. He was dressed in a simple, homespun loin cloth.

I knew him instantly, though he died twenty-five days after I was born. "Welcome, Bapu," I said. He smiled a gentle smile gave a slight bow with his hands pressed together, palms touching and fingers pointing upwards, thumbs close to the chest. In Hinduism it means "I bow to the divine in you."

Blessings to you kind Sir. I understand you are having issues with respect. Once, when I was younger and studying law at the University College of London, a white professor disliked me intensely and always displayed prejudice and animosity towards me.[1]

Because I never lowered my head when addressing him as he expected, there were always 'arguments' and confrontations. One day, the professor was having lunch at the dining room of the University, and I came along with my tray and sat next to the professor.[2]

The professor said, 'It appears, you do not understand. A pig and a bird do not sit together to eat.'[3]

I looked at him as a parent would a rude child and calmly replied, 'You do not worry professor. I'll fly away,' and I went and sat at another table. Reddened with rage, he decided to take revenge on the next test paper, but I responded well to all of the questions.[4]

The professor, unhappy and frustrated, asked me the following question. 'If you were walking down the street and found a package, and within was a bag of wisdom and another bag with a lot of money, which one would you take?'[5]

Without hesitating, I responded, 'The one with the money, of course.'[6]

The professor, smiling sarcastically said, 'I, in your place, would have taken the wisdom.'[7]

I shrugged indifferently and responded, 'Each one takes what he doesn't have.' By this time the professor was fit to be tied. So great was his anger that he wrote on my exam sheet the word 'idiot' and gave it to me.[8]

I took the exam sheet and sat down back at my desk, trying very hard to remain calm while I contemplated my next move.[9]

A few minutes later, I got up, went to the professor and said to him in a dignified but sarcastically polite tone, 'Sir, you autographed the sheet, but you did not give me the grade.' [10]

One should always be polite to another, but you do not have to treat disrespect with respect. Before you can respect another, you must respect yourself. In all things be polite but honest. [11]

He smiled a gentle smile and gave a slight bow and hands pressed together, palms touching and fingers pointing upwards, thumbs close to the chest. *I bow to the divine in you.* [12] He faded from sight but his words rang in my heart.

∞∞∞∞∞∞∞∞∞∞∞∞

"Grace is what picks me up and lifts my wings high above and I fly! Grace always conquers! Be graceful in everything; in anger, in sadness, in joy, in kindness, in unkindness, retain grace with you!

Elegance is a glowing inner peace. Grace is an ability to give as well as to receive and be thankful. Mystery is a hidden laugh always ready to surface! Glamour only radiates if there is a sublime courage and bravery within: glamour is like the moon; it only shines because the sun is there."[13]

Chapter Twenty-Seven

Strange as it is, I have always found relaxation in watching the flames of a fire or the movement of water. When we had our two-acre lake, during the winter it would freeze solid. Now, it is just a pond. Each year since we've been here, the lake freezes solid during the frigid winter.

Always at some point I've picked up a rock and thrown it on the ice to check the thickness of the ice and to see if it would crack. One day I learned it could make a sound.

Always before, the rocks would break through the ice with a "crack, splash" or, if the ice was really think, crash with a clunk and skitter across it. This particular day a fascinating thing happened. Instead of cracking or clunking, the fist-sized rock went "BOING."

It skidded across the ice with a "Boing, Boing, Boing, Boing" sound that was absolutely musical. Stronger and more resonant than a "Ding," not as deep as a "Gong," but not quite a "Dong."

Stunned, I picked up another rock and threw it. The "Boing, Boing, Boing, Boing" music sounded again in the still morning air. I did it yet again—Boing, Boing, Boing, Boing! Not once in the past had it made music and that music was wonderful.

Over the next few days, particularly in moments of stress, or boredom, I've "chunked" a couple of rocks. My reward... "Boing, Boing, Boing, Boing." A simple sound, but it has been mighty entertaining. I showed my "trick" to my wife; she giggled. All it takes is a frozen lake and a rock to chunk.

I don't have a scientific reason for the sound. My supposition is that the ice has formed almost a drum head, and if a slight gap exists between the ice and the top of the water, it will "Boing." But I'm not an "iceologist" or an acoustics expert, so I can't be sure.

Sometimes, you don't need to be sure of something, you just need to experience it. You see, you don't always need to figure out the "why"; you can just enjoy the "what" that results.

I wish my kids and grandkids could hear it, it is a truly beautiful sound. Maybe they will one day, even if it is not at my lake. After all, it only took me sixty-six years to hear it.

And on those occasions they will have to bundle up against the cold and the wind, or other challenges life puts in front of them, and do something silly just for the heck of it. Sometimes you might find yourself surprised by the reward God or nature or unexplained science grants you.

Maybe they will remember this story one day, I hope so. Maybe on a cold and blustery day sometime in their future, they will pick up a rock at throw it on a frozen pond.

But remember... to someone that pond might be their "lake." I hope they respect that premise more than the perspective.

Probably nothing will happen except the rock will simply crash and splash or clunk and skitter. I know that has been the case for me each winter for seven years.

But maybe, just maybe, it will "BOING," and for just a moment, they will smile and enjoy the music.

Maybe that smile will come from doing something they have done time after time after time and getting a new result.

An unexpected result, while it doesn't alter the universe, does bring a smile to your lips.

Maybe it will be trying something for the very first time and being successful at it. I really don't know which or either will be the case.

That's alright, the thing to remember is that, "Music is the silence between the notes."[1] Or in this case, the space between the "Boings."

After all, isn't that what magic is?

Grandfather Speaks Again

∞∞∞∞∞∞∞∞∞∞∞∞∞

*"All things of grace and beauty such that one holds
them to one's heart have a common provenance
in pain. Their birth in grief and ashes."*[2]

Chapter Twenty-Eight

[**guilt, a noun**. Responsibility for a crime or for doing something bad or wrong, a bad feeling caused by knowing or thinking that you have done something bad or wrong. The fact of having committed a breach of conduct especially violating law and involving a penalty; the state of one who has committed an offense especially consciously, feelings of culpability especially for imagined offenses or from a sense of inadequacy, a feeling of culpability for offenses.][1]

[**grace, a noun**. Simple elegance or refinement of movement, decency, (good) manners, politeness, decorum, respect, tact; (in Christian belief) the free and unmerited favor of God, as manifested in the salvation of sinners and the bestowal of blessings, a divinely given talent or blessing. The condition or fact of being favored by someone, favor, approval, approbation, acceptance, esteem, regard, respect.][2]

Suddenly Grandfather and I were sitting back in front of the campfire. "I have tried to have grace but I struggle with it," I admitted. "It seems so...

passive. I find I am more action-oriented. Some-times I feel guilty because of that."

What is this that you seek? What does grace mean to you? Grandfather asked.

"Grace has several meanings like simple ele-gance or refinement of movement, decency, good manners, politeness, decorum, respect, tact, the free and unmerited favor of God, as manifested in the salvation of sinners and the bestowal of bless-ings, a divinely given talent or blessing. The condi-tion or fact of being favored by someone, favor, approval, approbation, acceptance, esteem, regard and respect."[3]

I see. Your people use too many words to de-scribe one word. In Lakota Sioux the word is wóyawašte. It means blessing. In Cherokee it is adadolisdi, it means mercy, or sympathize. The Northern Inuit say saimarnert, meaning consolation.[4]

I find none of these to be passive; they re-quire much effort, much action and courage as does I suspect your word grace.

For the people, grace starts with inaction; for the moment, be still. Once you are still, the actions begin. The same is true for your peo-ple; first be still.

There is a saying among your people,[5] ***'Count the ways you are blessed. Be thankful.***

Be slow to quarrel. Search out a forgotten friend. Suspend suspicion, be trusting. Write a love letter. Share a treasure. Give a soft answer. Encourage youth.

'Show your loyalty in word and deed. Nourish a grateful attitude. Keep a promise. Find the time. Don't harbor a grudge. Listen. Apologize if you are wrong. Be understanding. Be slow to envy. Forgive. Think first of someone else. Show appreciation.

'Be kind. Count on miracles. Laugh more. Deserve confidence. Be gentle. Wage war against prejudice. Worship your God. Gladden the heart of a child. Decry complacency. Take pleasure in the beauty and wonder of the earth.

'Make every day a thanksgiving. Speak your gratitude. Speak it again. Speak it still again. Speak it still once more.'

"Why speak gratitude four times?"

Not just four, speak it often and with both peace and force, that way the Great Spirit is aware that you are aware of what he has given you.

I thought of a quote I once heard, "We often take for granted the very things that most deserve our gratitude."[6]

130

Grandfather Speaks Again

∞∞∞∞∞∞∞∞∞∞∞

"Grace doesn't depend on suffering to exist, but where there is suffering you will find grace in many facets and colors."[7]

Chapter Twenty-Nine

There are some things that are constant. These are things we can track our progress from and things we can navigate with.

"Grandfather, you mean like the 'ultimate truths' and constellations and the North Star?"

Truths yes, constellations I know not but I know the North Star. Do you know how it came to be?

"It just always has been there, right?"

He bowed his head and shook it. Looking up again there was great kindness in his eyes. Kindness for a student that did not understand how the world worked at all.

My Paiute brothers tell the story.[1] Long, long ago, when the world was young, the People of the Sky were so restless and travelled so much that they made trails in the heavens. Now, if we watch the sky all through the night, we can see which way they go.

But one star does not travel. That is the North Star. He cannot travel. He cannot move. When he was on the earth long, long ago, he was known as Na-gah, the mountain sheep, the son of Shinoh. He was brave, daring, sure-footed, and courageous.

His father was so proud of him and loved him so much that he put large earrings on the sides of his head and made him look dignified, important, and commanding.

Every day, Na-gah was climbing, climbing, climbing. He hunted for the roughest and the highest mountains, climbed them, lived among them, and was happy. Once in the very long ago, he found a very high peak.

Its sides were steep and smooth, and its sharp peak reached up into the clouds. Na-gah looked up and said, 'I wonder what is up there. I will climb to the very highest point.'

Around and around the mountain he travelled, looking for a trail. But he could find no trail. There was nothing but sheer cliffs all the way around. This was the first mountain Na-gah had ever seen that he could not climb.

He wondered and wondered what he should do. He felt sure that his father would feel ashamed of him if he knew that there was a mountain that his son could not climb.

Na-gah determined that he would find a way up to its top. His father would be proud to see him standing on the top of such a peak.

Again and again he walked around the mountain, stopping now and then to peer up the steep cliff, hoping to see a crevice on which he could find footing. Again and again, he went up as far as he could, but always had to turn around and come down.

At last he found a big crack in a rock that went down, not up. Down he went into it and soon found a hole that turned upward. His heart was made glad. Up and up he climbed.

Soon it became so dark that he could not see, and the cave was full of loose rocks that slipped under his feet and rolled down. Soon he heard a big, fearsome noise coming up through the shaft. At the same time the rolling rocks were dashed to pieces at the bottom.

In the darkness he slipped often and skinned his knees. His courage and determination began to fail. He had never before seen a place so dark and dangerous. He was afraid, and he was also very tired.

'I will go back and look again for a better place to climb,' he said to himself. 'I am not afraid out on the open cliffs, but this dark hole fills me with fear. I'm scared! I want to get out of here!'

But when Na-gah turned to go down, he found that the rolling rocks had closed the cave below him. He could not get down. He saw only one thing now that he could do; he *must go on climbing until he came out some-where.*

After a long climb, he saw a little light, and he knew that he was coming out of the hole. 'Now I am happy,' he said aloud. 'I am glad that I really came up through that dark hole.'

Looking around him, he became almost breathless, for he found that he was on the top of a very high peak! There was scarcely room for him to turn around, and looking down from this height made him dizzy.

He saw great cliffs below him, in every direction, and saw only a small place in which he could move. Nowhere on the outside could he get down, and the cave was closed on the inside...

'Here I must stay until I die,' he said. 'But I have climbed my mountain! I have climbed my mountain at last!'

He ate a little grass and drank a little water that he found in the holes in the rocks. Then he felt better. He was higher than any mountain he could see and he could look down on the earth, far below him.

About this time, his father was out walking over the sky. He looked everywhere for his son, but could not find him. He called loudly, 'Na-

gah! Na-gah!' And his son answered him from the top of the highest cliffs.

When Shinoh saw him there, he felt sorrowful, to himself, 'My brave son can never come down. Always he must stay on the top of the highest mountain. He can travel and climb no more.'

'I will not let my brave son die. I will turn him into a star, and he can stand there and shine where everyone can see him. He shall be a guide mark for all the living things on the earth or in the sky.'

And so Na-gah became a star that every living thing can see. It is the only star that will always be found at the same place. Always he stands still. Directions are set by him. Travelers, looking up at him, can always find their way.

He does not move around as the other stars do, and so he is called 'the Fixed Star.' And because he is in the true north all the time, our people call him Qui-am-i Wintook Poot-see. These words mean 'the North Star.'

Besides Na-gah, other mountain sheep are in the sky. They are called 'Big Dipper' and 'Little Dipper.' They too have found the great mountain and have been challenged by it.

They have seen Na-gah standing on its top, and they want to go on up to him.

Shinoh, the father of North Star, turned them into stars, and you may see them in the sky at the foot of the big mountain. Always they are travelling. They go around and around the mountain, seeking the trail that leads upward to Na-gah, who stands on the top. He is still the North Star.

"He had a dream and that dream trapped him… How sad," I said.

There is no sadness here; he lives on. He guides the people, he did what he set out to do. This is a story of great joy and purpose. Joy and purpose are the reason the Great Spirit has blessed mankind. They are his rewards.

I thought about it for a moment. "Are you saying I can be like the North Star? I can be the one to show the way, if I am consistent myself?"

Does not the North Star always point the way, even during the daylight when it can't be seen? It comes out each evening at darkness and walks across the sky. It remains, even though it cannot be seen. Always be the same my son, point the way even if no one wishes to go that direction.

∞∞∞∞∞∞∞∞∞∞∞

Why is being who you really are so hard for most people? Because they don't trust themselves enough.

Chapter Thirty

"But the brave's dream trapped him. I have dreams, how can I protect myself from them and not be trapped?"

All men dream, some dream good dreams, some dream bad dreams. Both can become reality if man is not careful. One can be a good thing that may have bad consequences. One is a bad thing that may have good benefits. It is up to man to decide. It is up to man to catch the bad dreams.

"How?"

My Lakota brothers tell the story of how you need a dream catcher.[1] Long ago when the world was young, an old Lakota spiritual leader was on a high mountain and had a vision. In his vision, Iktomi, the great trickster and teacher of wisdom, appeared in the form of a spider.

Iktomi spoke to him in a sacred language that only the spiritual leaders of the Lakota could understand. As he spoke Iktomi, the spider, took the elder's willow hoop which had feathers, horse hair, beads and offerings on it and began to spin a web.

He spoke to the elder about the cycles of life...and how we begin our lives as infants and we move on to childhood, and then to adulthood. Finally, we go to old age where we must be taken care of as infants, completing the cycle.

'But,' Iktomi said, as he continued to spin his web, 'in each time of life there are many forces—some good and some bad. If you listen to the good forces, they will steer you in the right direction. But if you listen to the bad forces, they will hurt you and steer you in the wrong direction.'

He continued, 'There are many forces and different directions that can help or interfere with the harmony of nature, and also with the Great Spirit and all of his wonderful teachings.'

All the while the spider spoke, he continued to weave his web starting from the outside and working towards the center. When Iktomi finished speaking, he gave the Lakota elder the web and said... 'See, the web is a perfect circle but there is a hole in the center of the circle.'

He said, 'Use the web to help yourself and your people to reach your goals and make use of your people's ideas, dreams and visions. If you believe in the Great Spirit, the web will catch your good ideas—and the bad ones will go through the hole.'

The Lakota elder passed on his vision to his people and now the Sioux Indians use the dream catcher as the web of their life. It is hung above their beds or in their home to sift their dreams and visions.

The good in their dreams are captured in the web of life and carried with them...but the evil in their dreams escapes through the hole in the center of the web and are no longer a part of them. They believe that the dream catcher holds the destiny of their future.

What do you believe, my son, about the destiny of your future?

I thought for a long moment. "I believe it is up to me to meet that destiny. I believe it is also up to me to maintain my own sanity as I go through this life. I should not allow others to weigh me down with their lacks... lacks of understanding, of commitment, or the inability to 'say what they mean and do what they say.' I cannot blame them because I am different, nor do I have to let them control me."

Very good. Now my son... I must leave you. The lessons are finished for this visit.

"Will you come back again, Grandfather?"

Will there be more to learn at another time? Probably. Will you remember all we have learned so far? Probably not. He laughed. ***My people have no word for goodbye; therefore, I'll say something I have heard you say. I will see you when I see you.***

∞∞∞∞∞∞∞∞∞∞∞

"Love people who hate you. Pray for people who have wronged you. It won't just change their life…it'll change yours."[2]

Chapter Thirty-One

As a writer, I realized Grandfather's and my other visitors' stories were full of metaphors, hyperboles and similes. His people needed them to tell stories; they did not have the language sophistication or technological tools to describe things as we do today.

English classes teach that a metaphor is based on comparison, some showing similarity but others showing differences. A hyperbole is based on exaggeration, both describing things that are literally impossible.

I thought about some common metaphor examples:[1] "Mary is a cold fish." Not literally a fish, but an unemotional person, devoid of temperament. "That guy is such a snake in the grass." "Her eyes were glowing coals." "That linebacker is a mountain."

Then hyperboles:[2] "Susan is as old as the hills." Meaning very old but no human can be literally as old as the hills. "Mark has scores of girlfriends," while in fact he may have three or four. Those two figures of speech can sometimes co-exist; if you say Mary is the coldest fish in the whole universe, that's metaphorical and hyperbolic at the same time.

A simile is a phrase that describes something in comparison to the characteristics of something else, usually using the words like or as. Some examples:[3] "He is as sneaky as a weasel." "A book is like a good meal." "Her teeth are like pearls."

The funny part is that even with our language sophistication and technology, we writers still use these tools to tell a story.

After all, a good story doesn't have to be true; it just has to be good.

∞∞∞∞∞∞∞∞∞∞∞

"I was working on the proof of one of my poems all the morning, and took out a comma. In the afternoon I put it back again."[4]

Chapter Thirty-Two

Do you understand that I was struggling with grace and revenge? That is why I had summoned Grandfather and the others, without being aware I had.

Have you ever wanted to say, "Today I made a decision, somehow I have to make you pay. No one makes a fool of me, no one ignores me without receiving retribution. No one hurts me for no reason and simply goes free. I want you in tears, never again to be the same. And you know what? It's just a matter of time.

"May you never rest easy again. 'To err is human, to forgive is divine.' I thought about forgiving you, but I want revenge. You have pissed me off for no reason. My rage is intoxicating, intimidating and invigorating. I want you reduced to nuclear ash so that on the next gentle breeze, you simply blow away."

I certainly have and it has rarely been said to my enemies.

I don't let my enemies get close. But I've come to know that it is your friends that will hurt you the worst. Usually, it will not even be for a good reason. It simply will be... and that is all. It will almost always be for something stupid and inconsequential... to them. As I pondered this, more thoughts came to mind:

"The greatest pleasure I know is to do a good deed by stealth and have it found out by accident."[1] Similar to random acts of kindness, I reasoned.

"The right time to show your good character is when you are pestered by somebody weaker than you."[2]

"The great gift of human beings is that we have the power of empathy."[3]

"You are never a loser until you quit trying."[4]

"When it is obvious that the goals cannot be reached, don't adjust the goals, adjust the action steps."[5]

After all, "Butterflies can't see their wings. They don't know how truly beautiful they are, but everyone else can. People are like that as well."[6]

Maybe I was being too hard on me...

"You can search throughout the entire universe for someone who is more deserving of your love and affection than you are yourself, and that person is not to be found anywhere."[7]

"Be kind, for everyone you meet is fighting a hard battle."[8]

It's been said, "Wisdom is the supreme part of happiness."[9]

"The moments of happiness we enjoy take us by surprise. It is not that we seize them, but that they seize us."[10]

Maybe the problem WAS me and I wasn't seizing those moments as well as I could have. What does grace mean to me?

First of all, I understand and accept that my religious readers will almost certainly place it in the "God category." I personally would prefer to remove that exclusivity from the discussion, but frankly... that will be difficult. Let me explain my position.

Grace to me is both a survival technique and a redemptive imperative, back in the "God category" I admit but... I believe that within the "course of human events" a man may redeem himself to other humans.

While redemption in the religious sense is in the purview of God, we still live with other humans. A simple apology may be sufficient for "simple sins," mistakes or mishaps but it also is a way to deflect the real purpose of redemption.

One of the more "famous of infamous" questions on personal health and redemption dealt with was the concept of a "superior being." How hard would it be to be superior to us?

It also acknowledged that different people may have different pictures of God. In spite of that, or maybe because of it, those ideas have worked for thousands of people. So here are the original twelve steps as published by Alcoholics Anonymous[11]:

1. We admitted we were powerless over alcohol—that our lives had become unmanageable.
2. Came to believe that a power greater than ourselves could restore us to sanity.
3. Made a decision to turn our will and our lives over to the care of God *as we understood Him.* (Italics mine.)

4. Made a searching and fearless moral inventory of ourselves.

5. Admitted to God, to ourselves, and to another human being the exact nature of our wrongs.

6. Were entirely ready to have God remove all these defects of character.

7. Humbly asked Him to remove our shortcomings.

8. Made a list of all persons we had harmed, and became willing to make amends to them all.

9. Made direct amends to such people wherever possible, except when to do so would injure them or others.

10. Continued to take personal inventory, and when we were wrong, promptly admitted it.

11. Sought through prayer and meditation to improve our conscious contact with God *as we understood Him*, praying only for knowledge of His will for us and the power to carry that out. (Italics mine.)

12. Having had a spiritual awakening as the result of these steps, we tried to carry this message to alcoholics, and to

practice these principles in all our affairs.

Final redemption is between the person and his/her God. It is predicated however on action steps. Things that must be done in the effort to redeem one's self to one's self and to others who have been harmed or injured by our own actions. It is from the aspect of redeeming one's self to one's self that I call it a survival technique.

Carrying anger, hate and a sense that "Damn it, I've been wronged and I want revenge" is not the way to go through life. At least for me it isn't. After a while I have found that it weakens me, distracts me and generally makes me feel like crap. Even when, "Damn it, I've been wronged and I want revenge." Much has been written about revenge:

"If you prick us do we not bleed? If you tickle us do we not laugh? If you poison us do we not die? And if you wrong us shall we not revenge?"[12]

"While seeking revenge, dig two graves—one for yourself."[13]

"Revenge is an act of passion; vengeance of justice. Injuries are revenged; crimes are avenged."[14]

"There is no revenge so complete as forgiveness."[15]

A little too esoteric for my taste. I prefer, "Living well really is the best revenge."[16]

I have learned that rarely do people apologize, and it is even rarer that they mean it if they do, and it is almost unheard of that they will modify their behavior. Without those things, the person is not able to "redeem" themselves with me.

Unless I want the hollowness of hurt feelings myself, I have determined that to survive I need to redeem myself to them. Never give to anger what stupidity should own...

Whether or not the person redeems his/her self with God is not my business. Whether or not the person redeems his/herself with themselves is not my business. I can only be responsible for me and I don't like the feelings I've carried because others did me wrong.

Grace cannot co-exist with rage and revenge; I've tried to do it. Here's the problem with my rage: I can't make that person pay. Anyone can make a fool of me, if I let them. Anyone can ignore me without receiving retribution, if I let them.

But no one can hurt me for no reason and simply go free. I really don't want them in tears, never again to be the same. I want them to be the friend they said they were but... were not. To be the person they claimed to be but... were not.

How many times have I thundered, "Yeah, I want revenge. You have pissed me off for no reason." Realizing that my rage is intoxicating, intimidating and invigorating AND it is poisonous to me. I should say to my offender, "I will not have you reduced to nuclear ash so that on the next gentle breeze, you simply blow away.

"Instead, I will forgive you, but know this... Forgiveness does not mean I will forget. You will not be allowed to do that to me again. THAT is within my power and within my responsibility. Have a good life, a great life. Be successful... simply know, whatever you can achieve, imagine or gain could have been so much more."

∞∞∞∞∞∞∞∞∞∞∞∞

"True friends stab you in the front."[17]

Chapter Thirty-Three

[**guilt, a noun**. Responsibility for a crime or for doing something bad or wrong, a bad feeling caused by knowing or thinking that you have done something bad or wrong. The fact of having committed a breach of conduct especially violating law and involving a penalty; the state of one who has committed an offense especially consciously, feelings of culpability especially for imagined offenses or from a sense of inadequacy, a feeling of culpability for offenses.][1]

What have I learned from these visits with Grandfather and his... my friends? From my pain?

- "My success or my failure is my responsibility. What I want is within my power if it only requires my effort and if I want it bad enough."[2]
- "Perspective is an individual opinion— change it and you change the world. You can choose to believe in something or nothing. You can choose to find magic in little things or turmoil in big things. It is my choice!"[3]
- "Magic is the fingerprint of God."[4]

- "The greatest gifts are the ones we give, not the ones we get."[5]
- "I am who I am not because of what happened to me, but because of how I chose to be and act after it happened."[6]
- "I should not cry because it is over, but smile because it happened."[7]
- "No one place I could find, no one person anywhere who had my answers—except the inner me I was afraid to trust."[8]
- "Anyone you want to keep in your life—never take for granted."[9]
- "When you have a handful of facts do not make them from ridiculous conclusions."[10]
- "One should not, one cannot, and one must not turn ones back on memory. Memory is not a morbid way of living. It is an exalted way of seeing one's life in its totality."[11]
- "Why was man created last? To be reminded, if he becomes haughty, that a mosquito came before him."[12]
- "You never have permanent friends or permanent enemies."[13]
- "Be careful when you find yourself believing what you want to believe. Right

now I need to wait, listen, look and learn. My willingness to choose is sufficient for now."[14]

- "The Power of Nothing is supreme. Patience is finding an acceptable alternative. Success is relative—so is failure."

- "Whatever is going to happen will happen. Be ready—be available—but be positive."[15]

- "Sometimes the only chance to win is to lose. Sometimes the only action is inaction. You can convince no one of anything but you may give them the freedom to convince themselves."

- "What then has more power than Nothing? See the omnipotence of nothingness. It encompasses all, overwhelms all, overpowers all. All that exists may be subdivided into its constituent parts. All save nothing. How do you divide nothing? How do you multiply it? Add to it? Its square root is nothing. Only by focusing on nothing can you perceive everything."[16]

- "Know without knowing, use the peripheral vision to allow response rather than reaction."[17]

- "Share—without proof, without answers, without questions—what greater commitment."[18]
- "If I am all I am—what else could I be?"
- "Our friends float past. We become involved with them, they float on, and we must rely on hearsay or lose track of them completely; they float back again we must either renew our friendship, catch up to date or find that they and we don't comprehend each other anymore."[19]

John Wayne played Ethan Edwards, the Marine Sergeant, John Striker, Davy Crockett, Rooster Cogburn and even Genghis Khan.

Tom Selleck played Matthew Quigley, Monica's boyfriend on *Friends*, Jesse Stone and now Frank Reagan.

Like them, each of us plays different roles: Husband, father, Wife, mother, Boss, friend, Warrior, benefactor, Brother, sister and Friend, friend.

Like actors, no role totally defines the actor. No role is the actor; rather the actor is each role.

So it is with friends, one day you lead, the next you follow. One day you're the subject matter expert, the next the student. Each role has its own dialog, each tells a particular story...

When the story is complete, the movie ends. Life goes on, until that final curtain we all face. The changes are easy if you remain consistent as a person. No one knows everything, no one is expected to. No one can do everything, no one is expected to.

There is no Academy Award for life; no Oscar. Being a friend is one of the hardest roles any of us play. Words and actions are open to interpretation, and misinterpretation; the benefits or consequences of each viewed and given a value by the other person. How that person interprets anything is based on their mood at the moment, honesty and respect.

Honesty and respect... foundations of a friendship. It should be expected that each friend will be honest, each friend will be truthful and honest, each friend to be there to prevent the other friend from being put in a bad place; an embarrassing place due to our actions... or inactions.

When that is allowed to happen, one friend has stopped being a friend to the other. Redemption at that point becomes a question of repentance... otherwise, sadly... the friendship dies.

∞∞∞∞∞∞∞∞∞∞∞∞

"An enemy can partly ruin a man,

but it takes a good-natured injudicious friend
to complete the thing and
make it perfect."[20]

Chapter Thirty-Four

Then there came another horse and rider, this time with the glint of armor flashing from both came up my driveway.

A red dragon showed on the white background on his shield. I was stunned to say the least. The horse snorted, restlessly; only the ornate reins and the strength of the rider kept it under control.

"Good day, Your Majesty," I said with a bow.

Good day Sir, am I correct thy need is great?

I shrugged. "I suppose one could say that. I assume you were directed here by a friend of mine?"

Aye, 'tis true. When we first met I thought him a Pict. I know him now as being from your world.

I smiled. "Majesty, at one time that was true, now he is a being from all worlds." The horse pawed at the ground, the rider sitting easy in the large saddle. His sword mounted on the left side of the saddle for a right handed draw.

The workmanship was... no words could describe it. After all, it had been "forged when the world was young, and bird and beast and flower

were one with man, and death was but a dream!"[1]
I wanted to touch it but dared not.

Aye, I think he more a brother of Merlin that either you or I. Able to come and go not as other men. A being of power and mystery. Pray tell me, Sir, how may I assist thee?

Humbled by the presence of yet another legend of time and hero of my youth, I also was embarrassed. "Your Majesty, I apologize for wasting your time. It is simply a loss of trust and respect I have suffered from the loss of another friend."

Tis the saddest of things, the loss of a friend. I lost the trust and respect of two: my wife and my best friend. Their passions overrode their love of me. No apology is necessary, Sir, not among those of us that have suffered such grievous losses.[2]

"I do not wish to pry... certainly it is not my business but I know your story well. Are you over the betrayal and if so... how did you get over it?"

I knew their hearts were pure and their love of me genuine, he said after a moment. *That did not ease the sting. But they were after all just people whose needs took precedence over their love and better glory.*

Am I over it? I don't know that one is ever over the pain, even when repentance is honestly made or when forgiveness is honestly given.

I surmise getting past it is sufficient for most men. After all before I was a king, I was a man. Before a knight, my friend was a man. Before a queen, my wife was a woman. We are but people, each.[3]

"So the stories are true. You and your Queen love again and your brother in arms rides at your side?"

The fault was not entirely theirs; I must accept some of it also. I did not protect them from themselves. Once, when I spoke to her I told her, I had often thought that in the hereafter of our lives, when I owe no more to the future and can be just a man, that we may meet, and she would come to me and claim me as hers, and know that I would be her husband. It was a dream I had... it is a dream that has become a reality.[4]

As to him, he was a Knight but first he was... but a man. He had pledged to love her always. He pledged to love her as his queen and as the wife of his best friend and as long as she lived... he would love no other. The weight of that love simply proved to heavy to carry. Especially, since it was returned.[5]

I bear as much guilt as they; I was King, a good king but not a good husband nor a good friend. I did not protect them from themselves. I did not see what was before me.[6]

It took the loss of my kingdom and my life for us to reclaim our honor and our loves.[7]

I pray Sir, such sacrifice not be laid on you. It is heavier than the world. Try to be at peace, attempt to find that peace before... before all is lost for there is no guarantee it can ever be found again.[8]

If thee can find that peace on this side of the darkness, thou hast a better chance to redeem yourself.[9]

"But I did nothing wrong. My anger is huge."

He smiled and gathered the reins back into his gloved hands. *So said I, Sir. So said I. I learned the hard way, the hardest way... I was wrong.*

If me, then why not you? I lost a kingdom, my life, my friend and my wife, I forgave. Pray tell me what you lost? Even The Christ on the cross forgave those killing him.[10]

You live. I told you there were things I did wrong, but could not see.[11]

Anger is but a poison, you give yourself. Ponder those words. Now, I must beg your leave. Now, once more, I must ride with my knights to defend what was, and the dream of what could be! Dreams are good. Good day Sir.[12]

"Wait Sire," I said. "One more question... when I first started having visitors like you, a fog would always roll in. The last few have come but the fog has not. Do you know why?"

The fog was never real, it was simply a way to focus your attention and soften the blow of meeting us.

Now, there is no need, the fog is gone because you no longer require it. You have done well, Sir, you are improving.

He wheeled the charge and the huge hooves beat a tattoo down my drive.

I whispered, "Good day, Your Majesty" and he was gone, faded back to... wherever he had come from. Camelot? The Dragon? History or legend? Did it even matter? Does it ever matter? Legend or reality, fact or fiction? Is there a difference; does it matter?

Then I heard a voice in the far distance, saying,

This is the oath of a Knight of King Arther's Round Table and should be for all of us to take to heart. I will develop my life for the greater good.[13]

I will place character above riches, and concern for others above personal wealth, I will never boast, but cherish humility instead, I will speak the truth at all times, and forever keep my word, I will defend those who cannot defend themselves, I will honor and respect women, and refute sexism in all its guises, I will uphold justice by being fair to all, I will be faithful in love and loyal in friendship, I will abhor scandals and gossip-neither partake nor delight in them, I will be generous to the poor and to those who need help, I will forgive when asked, that my own mistakes will be forgiven, I will live my life with courtesy and honor from this day forward.[14]

∞∞∞∞∞∞∞∞∞∞∞∞

"It is better to deserve honors and not have them than to have them and not to deserve them."[15]

Chapter Thirty-Five

My thoughts had settled, somewhat. Yet, it seemed a struggle was coming, not passing. I had something I had to do, something I would probably fail at. Something I would probably gain more pain from than relief.

Maybe it would work, maybe not. Maybe a friendship could be saved, maybe not... but there was only one way to find out.

I'd have to try.

A voice came to me on the wind, just a voice this time... ***I have waited until the last to speak to you. I'm at your service. You ask why and how and look for guarantees.***

***Why does the sun come up? Or are the stars just pin holes in the curtain of night, who knows? I know that you had no knowledge whatsoever of your potential. I know that because you were born different, men will fear you.*[1]**

You have competence and confidence and you will continue to intimidate those around you with less of either... or both.*[2] *There is nothing you can do about that but have patience. You have done well. But it'll take time. You are generations being born and dying. You

***are at one with all living things. Each man's
thoughts and dreams are yours to know. You
have the power of imagination. Use it well, my
friend.***[3]

I almost said, "Thank you, you Spanish pea-
cock," but remembered he was Egyptian.

*****

Later, Grandfather appeared again, standing near
the boulders and campfire. ***These have been your
truest friends—your heroes, my son. Be at
peace, but remember there will be more times
to sit with me and make talk and make smoke.
There is still much to learn.***

Someone, and I don't know who, said, "No family is perfect... we argue, we fight. We even stop
talking to each other at times. But in the end, family is family...The love will always be there." I hope
so...

∞∞∞∞∞∞∞∞∞∞

*"Reflect upon your present blessings, of which
every man has plenty; not on your past misfor-
tunes of which all men have some."*[4]

"Gratitude is riches. Complaint is poverty."[5]

Epilogue

Do I have any more answers? Maybe... but I know I have many more questions.

Like, what is the right way to sharpen a knife? I must rub it against something that is harder than the knife. I must have the right angle. I must balance the number of strokes on each side of the blade, or the edge will not be even. The same applies to us as people.

Find something or someone that is "harder" than you are and try your best to incorporate those good qualities into yourself.

Get the right "angle." That angle will always be how I can serve someone else, not myself. Find the "balance" by doing right things, the right way, every day.

Some people will come into my life and "sharpen" me by showing me how to live. Some people will come into my life and "sharpen" me by showing me how NOT to live. Both can teach me, one is just more fun than the other.

Next question. If I had a magic wand, what would I change in my life? I have often pondered the question. In the beginning, for years I contemplated what would I change if I could go back in time. What mistakes would I not make? What could I do to avoid hurting the people I have hurt? What disasters would I be able to avoid?

Then I came to realize that all of the things I would like to change or avoided or should have prevented were part of what has made me who I am today.

Everything that has come into my life—every friend, every enemy, every opportunity, every failure, every accomplishment, every embarrassment, every goal achieved and every goal denied—have all worked together to make me exactly who I am at this moment.

This is particularly true of those things that I would consider negative in my life.

I learned that I could lie, cheat, steal, lust, betray friends and seek comfort from my enemies. I have learned that integrity is only integrity as long as it is protected and defended. I have learned that fear can be a friend; it keeps me from being stupid.

I have learned that courage is not the absence of fear; rather it is the controlling of that fear.

In the "old days," bad things happened to good people. People were expected and required to "get past" those bad things. Previous generations recognized that individual events were a poor standard by which to evaluate life. Invariably, people grew stronger for having combated the negative forces they encountered.

We discovered that the "combat fatigue" experienced by soldiers during World War II and previous conflicts was better namcd "Post Traumatic Shock Syndrome," and then "Post Traumatic Stress Disorder." I never figured out which was worse; syndrome or disorder.

My Dad, like many soldiers from World War II, saw horrific things. He felt fear, he saw friends killed in front of his own eyes. He carried those images with him until the day he died; but he, like many other men and women who are placed in traumatic conditions, did his very best to "get past" those isolated and terrible events.

He decided that he would not let those terrible events define his life; rather, he would use those terrible events to help **refine** his life.

There was no way to stop the visions, but he learned to deal with them as dreams, horrible memories, but just that—memories.

You see it is a condition of living that we humans will suffer. It is also a condition of living that we humans will fail. It is a condition of living that terrible things will happen that can affect us for a long time.

It is also a condition of living that we humans will prevail.

It is a condition of living that we humans will succeed.

It is a condition of living that wonderful things will happen that can affect us for a long time.

Memory is a magical thing. A song, a scent or a sight can instantly transport a human mind through days, years or decades to a previous event. And while the human mind explores the reliving of that event, the event is almost real again.

The operative phrase is "almost."

John Wayne said, "Tomorrow is the most important thing in life. Comes into us at midnight very clean. It's perfect when it arrives and it puts itself in our hands. It hopes we've learned something from yesterday."

What will tomorrow bring for me and my friends? I have hunted for the right words; so far in vain. Mark Twain said, "The difference between the right word and the almost right word is the difference between lightning and a lightning bug. The right word may be effective, but no word was ever as effective as a rightly timed pause." So, I pause...

Legend says as Buddha lay on his death bed surrounded by his disciples, he said simply, "Do your best." Is this not all any of us can do?

Our only real danger is in picking our friends.

Grandfather Speaks Again

*"We can only be said to be alive in those moments
when our hearts are conscious
of our treasures."*[1]

Author's Note

Dear Reader,

Life has a way of happening and sometimes, you are simply along for the ride!

When I started this story, it was about lost friendships. I thought I had finished writing this story, but I was wrong. The story had not ended, I just didn't know it yet.

There is an "arrogant humility" I feel sometimes as a writer. When I want to tell a story I want it to be a good story, a story with a message. The arrogance is I think I'm good enough to tell it; the humility is that I can only hope I am.

When a story bites hold of me, it will not leave me alone until it has been told. This story grabbed me like that and wouldn't turn loose. The truth is, this story led me to a greater story.

I know since it happened to me, I'm the only one that can write it; hopefully I'm good enough to tell the story...

It was in the late 1970s, while we were both still on active duty with the Air Force, that I met Jim. Almost immediately I started calling him Mongo and he started calling me Junior. He was one of the strongest, hardest men I ever knew; and one of the gentlest. Most folks never saw that last side of him, but I did. Mongo was... difficult for some people to deal with. One side of him was the engineer, "Facts, Ma'am, just give me the facts." The other side... well like I said, most folks didn't get to see that side.

For the next several years, he was a steady fixture in my family, my job, my life. He was my guide, sometimes my teacher... he was a yard stick I measured myself against. Someone I wanted to be more like. He was my friend.

But life has a way of happening and sometimes, you are simply along for the ride!

The last time I saw him was twenty-eight years ago; the last time we had spoken was in 2003.

I lost him for all of those years I carried guilt that somehow I had offended him. For all of those years, I missed him. For all of those years, the feeling of loss sometimes angered me, sometimes humbled me, sometimes shattered me, but the feelings never left.

Life has a way of happening and sometimes, you are simply along for the ride!

Life took a turn; something happened I feel you as my readers need to know about. Although, frankly, if you have not experienced something similar, you probably won't comprehend it fully.

It was a Friday in February 2015 when my daughter, Shelley, called to tell me Mongo's wife, Mary, had died. I knew Mary; I remember when Mongo fell in love with her... I remember Mary had already fallen in love with him; he just didn't know it. Engineer side, remember. She also changed his name, he wasn't Mongo anymore or even Jim. He became J.T.

She was a gentle soul, but a force of nature at the same time. That rare mix of good looks, sharp mind, determination, grace, and drive. Mary simply refused to settle... on anything, especially the status quo. She knew how to live, how she wanted to live and she knew what it would take to make her happy and it was called J.T.

Back to the story, it took four days before Shelley was able to locate phone numbers for his step-son, John, or one for Mongo. John had been one of my karate students; sweet kid.

Trepidation and anxiety threatened to smother me. I called John first. I explained I did not know how or even if my old friend would accept a call from me, and I did not want to intrude in what I felt had to be a devastating time in his life. John said, "Call him."

Working up my courage, I dialed the number. When Mongo answered the phone, I gave him my sympathies. I gave him a humble, sincere apology for whatever I had done to offend him. I told him I didn't want my presence to be a problem for him at a time like this. Then I asked his permission to attend the visitation and funeral.

He said, "Bob, there has never been a problem between us. Our lives just went in different directions."

I cannot describe the cacophony of feelings those two sentences gave me. Freedom from the mystery and guilt. Redemption. Hope for the future. Light in the darkness. None of these explain it but all were part of the music.

Several days later, I walked into the funeral home in Winnfield, Louisiana. The nine plus hour drive had been unsettling to say the least. But the 400 or so steps from my car to the door of the viewing room were some of the most uncomfortable I've ever walked.

Then, there he was.

When he stood, I saw my old friend. Older, grayer... my friend. But here's the point of this story—my gift to you, my readers. I saw a man during one of the most devastating and crippling times a man has to live through; the death of his wife.

But I was not seeing a devastated or crippled man.

I saw a man that finally had found everything he had looked for during the early days of our friendship. A man that was more "completed" than I had ever seen. A man that had truly been transformed by the love of a good woman, and a gracious, loving God.

Now, as I write this to you... the visitation is over, the funeral is passed. Mary has been laid to rest. Today he is driving back to their home in Texas; there will probably be no one else in the car. But, he will not be alone. There will be times probably when he will be lonely I'm sure. But he will never be alone. He carries her with him, as she carried him to completion.

Since that first meeting and during the days before I wrote this for you, my reader, I have struggled with adjectives. I, a writer, someone who plays with words, was completely unable to fully describe what had happened. Even to myself.

Amazing.
Stunned.
Beautiful.
Sad.
Peaceful.
Strange.
Graceful.
Remarkable.

Stunning and graceful seem to be the ones I keep coming back too. The closest one I settled on was again, complete.

While there was sadness, there was joy. Sadness, she had left; joy her suffering had ended. Sadness and joy, swirling around, through and throughout those forty-eight hours.

Sadness, he was alone, again. Joy, her touch was still in his life and heart and soul. Sadness, she had left; joy and a certainty they would be together again...

During the visitation, her son John came up to me, twenty-years missing between us also; there stood a young man. Now taller than me, I looked hard to see him. In the movie *Hook*, Peter Pan had grown up and forgotten who he was.

I remembered the scene when one of the lost boys took the grown up Peter's face in his hands and moved Peter's head around before saying, "There you are Peter, I can see you." I did the same thing to John, even calling him Peter.

The sweet, knuckle-headed, young boy I remembered... he was still in there. But now in the body of a man. A really good man with a lovely wife and daughters. I treasured meeting them.

A while back, I had seen Kevin, Mongo's stepson from his first marriage. The two had lost touch with each other a while back. Life has a way of happening and sometimes, you are simply along for the ride.

Kevin's family was there, beautiful wife, lovely daughters and a son named J.T., who was a carbon copy of Kevin at that age. There was Kevin's sister, Jeri.

It must have taken Mary's death to have that contact re-established. Mary would have been pleased, because she never settled for the status quo. Her daughter Wendy found Kevin and Jeri for J.T.

Oh, and Mary's brother Richard... as one of the officiators for her funeral, finally got the last word on Mary and proclaimed it to the congregation. That, of course, will only last until they meet again.

*****

My thoughts swirled all the way back home and even after I arrived. I realized that over the years I had met other "completed" people. But I met them only AFTER they had been completed. Never had I seen someone I knew... I had lived with... I had walked down the path of joys and devastation with... BECOME completed... Never... until now.

Life has a way of happening and sometimes, you are simply along for the ride!

His life had happened; I was not there to see it. He had found "IT", I had not been there to experience it. He had been redeemed, I was not there to watch it. He had been completed, I did not know it... until now.

We had shared some of the worse things either of us had to live through; we had missed many of the truly great things life gave us.

Life has a way of happening and sometimes, you are simply along for the ride.

I don't know what will happen with our friendship, but whatever it will be... it will not be what it was. I don't know if there will be room for me in J.T.'s world, I do know there will not be the "need" that used to be. How could there be. He is completed.

Maybe there will be space that on occasion we can share. I'm good with that. Maybe there will not be and I'm good with that also. After all, he is completed. Mongo is gone, that's hard for me to accept; but I'm really hoping to get to know J.T.

Now, Reader, to the reason I share it with you. Of the three damaged friendships that started this book, two are unchanged. But the third! Here is my gift to you Reader, HOPE... If J.T. found this completion, another person could. If J.T. searched those long years and found it, another person can.

Most important is if you are searching for it... you can.

I have seen one of the strongest men I have ever known, strengthened beyond imagination. I have seen one of the hardest men I have ever known, softened.

Not weakened; like well-made steel, he was simply... properly tempered. He is better, not lessened. Stronger, not weaker. Found, not lost.

He kept searching for what he knew was out there and found more than he ever dreamed was possible. Among these, peace and grace...

Reader, be at peace but continue to search... Challenge anything and everything, but be graceful. Neither fight the truth or for the truth; you already have it.

Richard Bach said in his book *Illusions: The Adventures of a Reluctant Messiah*, "No one place I could find, no one person anywhere had my answers—except the inner me I was afraid to trust."

Trust you... believe in you... I do. But, if you do not believe in magic you will not see it when it happens. You will call it a coincidence; there aren't any. Oh, and don't let my use of the word magic upset you. Magic is simply the fingerprint of God.

Now, the clincher... though you will seek, the truth is you won't find "IT". The real magic is "IT" will find you... AND it already has. You just don't know it yet.

There IS a place where X truly does mark the spot... where there will be treasure and no more dragons and demons.

Sadly, you may be standing on it and don't see the X. Hint: You may have to get down on your knees to see it.

I know the X is real, you can either say J.T. found "IT" or "IT" found him. The important part is, being found. He was...

Life has a way of happening and sometimes... on occasion... it truly is a remarkable ride.

∞∞∞∞∞∞∞∞∞∞

"There are only two ways to live your life. One is as though nothing is a miracle. The other is as though everything is a miracle."[1]

Author's Parting Thoughts

As you can tell, I spent a great amount of energy on the Heroes. Unfortunately, many or most readers under 55-60 years old may have very little exposure to the ones I used. The point is this; we need heroes as friends but not necessarily the ones I used. They are from my timeline; yours may be different.

Let us remember for example, Sgt Preston of the Yukon for our Canadian friends, or the Shadow, Green Hornet, Captain Marvel, Zorro, Hercules, Batman, Spiderman, Incredible Hulk, Ironman, Flash, Wolverine, Captain America, Ghost Rider, Superboy, X-Men, Fantastic Four, and Thor. Superman has been popular with all generations since the mid 30's. Let us not forget the ladies, either, which included Supergirl, Wonder Woman, Cat Woman, Elektra and Batgirl. Nor, the Avengers. They are all heroes. They are all friends. That is the important part to remember.

Identify your own heroes: a teacher, a friend, a soldier, a police officer, a fireman, your mom or your dad... maybe your brother or sister. Who knows; heroes come in different shapes, sizes, colors and genders for different people.

About Grandfather's Friends

Chapter Six[1]

John Bernard Books, played by John Wayne in the 1976 western film *The Shootist*, which would prove to be John Wayne's final film role. The picture is about a dying gunfighter who spends his last days looking for a way to die with the least pain and the most dignity.

Chapter Eight

My Dad, Marvin "Buddy" Anderson. The hardest man I ever knew. The smartest man I ever knew. The best Sergeant I ever knew. My hero. The sad part is I didn't really know him until he had been dead for many years. Then I began to understand so much I never understood before—it was just a matter of time.

Chapter Eleven[2]

Roy Rogers was an American actor and singer best known as the "King of the Cowboys" for his heroic roles in musical Westerns. His sidekick palomino, Trigger, and dog, Bullet often appeared with him. Born on November 5, 1911, in Cincinnati, Ohio, he was known as the "King of the Cowboys." Starring in musical Westerns, he appealed to fans for his good-guy hero image. Rogers appeared on TV, radio, records and film from the 1930s to 1950s. He died on July 6, 1998, from congestive heart failure.

Chapter Twelve
Merlin, wizard to Arthur. I used to think that Lancelot was "the man." Then I learned about Arthur and decided he was "the man." I was wrong, "the man" was Merlin. Without him nothing would have happened, nor would it have been remembered.

Chapters Fourteen, Fifteen and Sixteen
Tinkerbell, Peter Pan's mystical fairy friend. Beautiful beyond description. Impossible to hold... Demanding, delightful... and you must believe in fairies or she and the other fairies will die.

Chapter Nineteen
Muffin, Buddha, Jack Daniels, and Gibson, our former pet dog companions. What can I tell you about them? Each was so unique, each personality so different. Muffin came first. I found her soaking wet on the side of the road; a runaway. Buddha came next and left us first. An old soul and Muffin's soul mate. Jack, my "lion" dog, spent most of his time "lying" around the house. But he

was an explorer at heart. Gibson, sweet gentle Gibson... smarter than me, more gentle than Pam. He was the glue that held us together for a while. Each was a better friend than most people I know.

Chapter Twenty-Two[3]
William Barclay "Bat" Masterson was born November 26, 1853 and died October 25, 1921. He was a figure of the American Old West known as a buffalo hunter, U.S. Marshal and Army scout. In later life he was a sports editor and columnist for the *New York Morning Telegraph*. The story that he needed to carry a cane for the rest of his life is a legend perpetuated by the NBC TV series ***Bat Masterson***, starring Gene Barry that ran from 1958 to 1961.

Bat lived during a violent and frequently lawless period. The fact that he was so widely known can be ascribed to a practical joke played on a gullible newspaper reporter in August 1881. Later, he worked as a sports writer and editor, and a columnist. It was during this time that he sold his famous six gun because he 'needed the money.' Masterson allegedly bought old guns at pawnshops, carved notches into the handles and sold them. Each time he claimed the gun was the one he used during his career as a lawman.

Chapter Twenty-Four[4]

Paladin from ***Have Gun – Will Travel*** was an American Western television series that aired on CBS from 1957 through 1963. The main character, played by Richard Boone, was known only as Paladin a black garbed gun fighter that used philosophy and intelligence more than his .45. In season 2, Episode 12, The Ballad of Oscar Wilde, Paladin met Oscar Wilde. Quotes attributed to Wilde in this work are not from that episode but from public domain sources of Wilde's quotes. ***Have Gun—Will Travel*** was rated number three or number four in the Nielsen ratings every year of its first four seasons. It was one of the few television shows to spawn a successful radio version. Twenty four of the 225 episodes were written by Gene Roddenberry, the creator of Star Trek.

Paladin was the only western hero to have a business card.

Chapter Twenty-Six[5]

Mohandas Karamchand Gandhi was born 2 October 1869 and was the preeminent leader of Indian independence movement in British-ruled India. He was called by the honorific Mahatma which means 'high-souled' or 'venerable.' He was also called Bapu, an: endearment for 'father' or 'papa' in India. He died 30 January 1948. He lived modestly in a self-sufficient residential community and wore the traditional Indian dhoti, loin cloth and shawl, woven with hand spun yarn.

Chapter Thirty-Four

King Arthur, —Arthur... real? Imagined? Amalgamation? What difference does it make. He is the "once and future King". Owner of the Round table, "Right makes might," and so much more. A man whose story is known by many, a lesson for some, a damnation for others.

King Arthur and Merlin from *Excalibur,* a 1981 dramatic fantasy film directed, produced and co-written by John Boorman. It retold the legend of King Arthur and Guinevere, the Knights of the Round Table and Merlin and got its name from the legendary sword of King Arthur.[6]

Chapter Thirty-Five[7]

Juan Sánchez Villa-Lobos Ramírez is a fictional character in the **Highlander** film series. He was portrayed by Sean Connery. He was an Immortal, born in Egypt, by 1541, he was living in Spain, working as the Chief Metallurgist to King Charles V. That was when he contacted Conner MacLeod. Ramírez appeared in **Highlander, Highlander II; The Quickening**, and was mentioned in **Highlander; The Series**. Other than James Bond, Ramírez is the only character that Connery has played in more than one film.

Notes

Chapter One

1. www.oxforddictionaries.com/us
2. www.oxforddictionaries.com/us
3. www.oxforddictionaries.com/us
4. *Holy Bible: New International Version*, 2 Corinthians 9:8

Chapter Two
1. www.oxforddictionaries.com/us
2. C. Joy Bell

Chapter Three
1. Robert Goolrick, *The End of the World as We Know It: Scenes from a Life*

Chapter Four
1. Richard Bach, *Illusions: The Adventures of a Reluctant Messiah*
2. Richard Bach, *Illusions: The Adventures of a Reluctant Messiah*
3. Margaret Peterson Haddix, *Into the Gauntlet*

Chapter Five
1. www.Oxforddictionaries.com/us

2. Matthew Henry, *Matthew Henry's Commentary on the Whole Bible: Complete and Unabridged in One Volume*

Chapter Six

1. Quote by John Bernard Books from the movie The Shootist. www.IMBD.com
2. Quote by Davy Crockett from the movie The Alamo. www.IMBD.com
3. Quote by John Bernard Books from the movie The Shootist. www.IMBD.com
4. Quote by John Bernard Books from the movie The Shootist. www.IMBD.com
5. Anne Lamott, *Traveling Mercies: Some Thoughts on Faith*

Chapter Seven

1. www.Wikipedia.com
2. www.Oxforddictionaries.com/us
3. www.Wikipedia.com
4. www.Wikipedia.com
5. www.Wikipedia.com
6. www.Wikipedia.com
7. www.Wikipedia.com
8. www.Wikipedia.com
9. www.Wikipedia.com
10. www.Wikipedia.com
11. www.Wikipedia.com

12. www.Wikipedia.com

13. www.Wikipedia.com

14. www.Wikipedia.com

15. www.Wikipedia.com

16. www.Wikipedia.com

17. www.Wikipedia.com

18. www.Wikipedia.com

19. www.Wikipedia.com

20. www.Wikipedia.com

21. Anne Lamott, *Traveling Mercies: Some Thoughts on Faith*

Chapter Eight

1. The Difference Between Military Friends and Civilian Friends. Public domain information.

2. The Difference Between Military Friends and Civilian Friends. Public domain information.

3. The Difference Between Military Friends and Civilian Friends. Public domain information.

4. The Difference Between Military Friends and Civilian Friends. Public domain information.

5. The Difference Between Military Friends and Civilian Friends. Public domain information.

6. The Difference Between Military Friends and Civilian Friends. Public domain information.

7. The Difference Between Military Friends and Civilian Friends. Public domain information.

8. The Difference Between Military Friends and Civilian Friends. Public domain information.

9. The Difference Between Military Friends and Civilian Friends. Public domain information.

10. The Difference Between Military Friends and Civilian Friends. Public domain information.

11. Anne Morrow Lindbergh

Chapter Nine

1. www.Wikipedia.com

2. C.S. Lewis, *The Four Loves*

3. Hermann Hesse, *Siddhartha*

Chapter Ten

1. www.Wikipedia.com

2. Gerald Lawson Sittser, *A Grace Disguised: How the Soul Grows Through Loss*

Chapter Eleven

1. Stanza 1 of Tumbling Tumbleweeds. Public domain information.

2. Stanza 2 of Tumbling Tumbleweeds. Public domain information.

3. www.HappyTrails.org (Roy Rogers)

4. www.HappyTrails.org (Roy Rogers)

5. www.Wikipedia.com

6. www.Wikipedia.com

7. www.Wikipedia.com

8. Stanzas 3, 4 and 5 of Tumbling Tumble-weeds. Public domain information.

9. Simone Weil, *Gravity and Grace*

Chapter Twelve

1. Quote by Merlin from the movie Excalibur. www.IMBD.com

2. Quote by Merlin from the movie Excalibur. www.IMBD.com

3. Quote by Merlin from the movie Excalibur. www.IMBD.com

4. Quote by Merlin from the movie Excalibur. www.IMBD.com

5. Quote by Merlin from the movie Excalibur. www.IMBD.com

6. Quote by Merlin from the movie Excalibur. www.IMBD.com

7. Quote by Merlin from the movie Excalibur. www.IMBD.com

8 Quote by Merlin from the movie Excalibur. www.IMBD.com

9. Quote by Merlin from the movie Excalibur. www.IMBD.com

10. Catullus

Chapter Thirteen

1. Attributed to Jacqueline Winspear

Chapter Fourteen
1. Bob Anderson, *Anderson's Rules*
2. C. Joy Bell

Chapter Fifteen
1. Bob Anderson, *Anderson's Rules*
2. C. Joy Bell

Chapter Sixteen
1. Bob Anderson, *Anderson's Rules*
2. Dr. Seuss
3. Bob Anderson, *Anderson's Rules*
4. Bob Anderson, *Anderson's Rules*
5. Quote from movie *Peter Pan,* "Peter Pan" by J.M. Barrie. www.IMBD.com
6. Robert A. Heinlein

Chapter Seventeen
1. Bob Anderson, *Anderson's Rules*
2. Bob Anderson, *Anderson's Rules*
3. Bob Anderson, *Anderson's Rules*
4. Bob Anderson, *Anderson's Rules*
5. Bob Anderson, *Anderson's Rules*
6. Bob Anderson, *Anderson's Rules*
7. Bob Anderson, *Anderson's Rules*
8. Bob Anderson, *Anderson's Rules*
9. Paul Murray, *Skippy Dies*

Chapter Eighteen
1. Marilynne Robinson, *Gilead*

Chapter Nineteen
1. Milan Kundera

Chapter Twenty
1. Max Lucado, *Max on Life: Answers and Insights to Your Most Important Questions*

Chapter Twenty-One
1. Beth Norman Harris (wall handing in veterinarian office)
2. George Bird Evans, *Troubles with Bird Dogs*
3. Ann Landers
4. Ann Landers
5. Will Rogers
6. Unknown Author
7. Andy Rooney
8. Mark Twain
9. Sigmund Freud
10. James Thurber
11. Elizabeth Gilbert, *Eat, Pray, Love*

Chapter Twenty-Two
1. www.Wikipedia.com
2. www.Wikipedia.com

3. Bernard Meltzer
4. Fr. Jerome Cummings
5. Cindy Lew
6. Elbert Hubbard
7. Aristotle
8. Abraham Lincoln
9. Anonymous
10. Hasidic Saying
11. Walter Winchell
12. Anonymous
13. James Boswell, 1763
14. Euripides, 408 B.C.
15. Solomon Ibn Gabirol
16. Samuel Johnson
17. Marlene Dietrich
18. Len Wein
19. Jan Wilson, *What is Friendship?* http://www.cyberparent.com/friendship/whatis-friendshipdefined.htm
20. Ralph Waldo Emerson
21. www.Wikipedia.com
22. Theme song from TV Show, Bat Masterson. www.wikipedia.com.
23. Mark Twain

Chapter Twenty-Three
1. www.Wikipedia.com
2. www.Wikipedia.com

3. www.Oxforddictionaries.com/us

4. www.Oxforddictionaries.com/us

5. Flannery O'Connor, *Mystery and Manners: Occasional Prose*

Chapter Twenty-Four

1. Quote by Paladin from Have Gun—Will Travel. www.IMDB.com

2. Quote by Paladin from Have Gun—Will Travel. www.IMDB.com

3. Quote by Paladin from Have Gun—Will Travel. www.IMDB.com

4. Quote by Paladin from Have Gun—Will Travel. www.IMDB.com

5. Quote by Paladin from Have Gun—Will Travel. www.IMDB.com

6. Quote by Paladin from Have Gun—Will Travel. www.IMDB.com

7. Quote by Paladin from Have Gun—Will Travel. www.IMDB.com

8. Quote by Paladin from Have Gun—Will Travel. www.IMDB.com

9. Quote by Paladin from Have Gun—Will Travel. www.IMDB.com

10. Quote by Paladin from Have Gun—Will Travel. www.IMDB.com

11. Quote by Paladin from Have Gun—Will Travel. www.IMDB.com

12. Quote by Paladin from Have Gun—Will Travel. www.IMDB.com

13. Charles Portis, *True Grit*

Chapter Twenty-Five

1. Shannon L. Alder
2. Anuj Somany
3. Jackie Robinson
4. Gary Chapman
5. Judith McNaught
6. Amit Kalantri
7. Lancelot
8. Khalil Gibran
9. C.S. Lewis
10. Buddha
11. Robert Brault
12. Ally Condie
13. Jess C. Scott
14. John O'Donohue

Chapter Twenty-Six

1. Story about Mahatma Gandhi, Public domain information.

2. Story about Mahatma Gandhi, Public domain information.

3. Story about Mahatma Gandhi, Public domain information.

4. Story about Mahatma Gandhi, Public domain information.

5. Story about Mahatma Gandhi, Public domain information.

6. Story about Mahatma Gandhi, Public domain information.

7. Story about Mahatma Gandhi, Public domain information.

8. Story about Mahatma Gandhi, Public domain information.

9. Story about Mahatma Gandhi, Public domain information.

10. Story about Mahatma Gandhi, Public domain information.

11. Story about Mahatma Gandhi, Public domain information.

12. Mahatma Gandhi

13. C. Joy Bell

Chapter Twenty-Seven
1. Claude Debussy
2. Cormac McCarthy, *The Road*

Chapter Twenty-Eight
1. www.Oxforddictionaries.com/us
2. www.Oxforddictionaries.com/us

3. www.Oxforddictionaries.com/us

4. www.Wikipedia.com

5. Thanksgiving saying. Public domain information.

6. Cynthia Ozick

7. Wm. Paul Young, *The Shack: Where Tragedy Confronts Eternity*

Chapter Twenty-Nine

1. Why The North Star Stands Still. Public domain information.

Chapter Thirty

1. The Legend of the Dream Catcher. Public domain information.

2. Mandy Hale

Chapter Thirty-One

1. Metaphor examples, www.Answers.com

2. Hyperbole examples, www.Answers.com

3. Simile examples, www.Answers.com

4. Oscar Wilde

Chapter Thirty-Two

1. Charles Lamb

2. Buddha

3. Meryl Streep

4. Mike Ditka

5. Confucius

6. Anonymous

7. Buddha

8. Philo

9. Sophocles

10. Ashley Montague

11. http://alcoholicsanonymous.com/aa-12-step-program-alcoholics-anonymous/

12. William Shakespeare

13. Credited to Douglas Horton

14. Samuel Johnson

15. Josh Billings

16. George Herbert, the English metaphysical poet and Clergyman

17. Oscar Wilde

Chapter Thirty-Three

1. www.Oxforddictionaries.com/us

2. Bob Anderson, *Anderson's Rules*

3. Bob Anderson, *Anderson's Rules*

4. Bob Anderson, *Anderson's Rules*

5. Bob Anderson, *Anderson's Rules*

6. Bob Anderson, *Anderson's Rules*

7. Dr. Seuss

8. Richard Bach, *Bridge Across Forever*

9. Richard Bach

10. Unknown

11. Elie Weisel
12. Mark Twain
13. Henry Kissinger
14. Unknown
15. Unknown
16. Unknown
17. Martial Arts Saying, Author unknown
18. Martial Arts Saying, Author unknown
19. John Barth, *The Floating Opera* Novel
20. Mark Twain

Chapter Thirty-Four

1. Partial quote by King Arthur from the movie Excalibur. www.IMDB.com

2. Partial quote by King Arthur from the movie Excalibur. www.IMDB.com

3. Partial quote by King Arthur from the movie Excalibur. www.IMDB.com

4. Partial quote by King Arthur from the movie Excalibur. www.IMDB.com

5. Partial quote by King Arthur from the movie Excalibur. www.IMDB.com

6. Partial quote by King Arthur from the movie Excalibur. www.IMDB.com

7. Partial quote by King Arthur from the movie Excalibur. www.IMDB.com

8. Partial quote by King Arthur from the movie Excalibur. www.IMDB.com

9. Partial quote by King Arthur from the movie Excalibur. www.IMDB.com

10. Partial quote by King Arthur from the movie Excalibur. www.IMDB.com

11. Partial quote by King Arthur from the movie Excalibur. www.IMDB.com

12. King Arthur, Le Morte d'Arthur: King Arthur and the Legends of the Round Table. www.goodreads.com/work/quotes/1361856-le-morte-d-arthur

13. Partial quote by King Arthur from the movie Excalibur. www.IMDB.com

14. Partial quote by King Arthur from the movie Excalibur. www.IMDB.com

15. Oscar Wilde

Chapter Thirty-Five

1. Quote by Juan Sanchez Villa-Lobos Ramirez from the movie Highlander. www.IMDB.com.

2. Bob Anderson, *Anderson's Rules*

3. Partial quote by Juan Sanchez Villa-Lobos Ramirez from the movie Highlander. www.IMDB.com.

4. Charles Dickens

5. Doris Day

Epilogue:
1. Thornton Wilder

Author's Note:
1. Albert Einstein

About Grandfather's Friends
1. www.Wikipedia.com
2. www.Wikipedia.com
3. www.Wikipedia.com
4. www.Wikipedia.com
5. www.Wikipedia.com
6. www.Wikipedia.com
7. www.Wikipedia.com

About the Author

Bob is a speaker and avid writer. As a speaker, his power message advocates doing hard things, especially when it's unpopular or uncomfortable to do so; simple and back to basics. He believes in unwavering commitment and courage. He believes success is earned, not given; it's a privilege, not a right.

Bob retired as a Chief Master Sergeant from the United States Air Force Reserve (USAFR) with over 32 years of service.

He is co-author of **The Survivalist** series with Jerry and Sharon Ahern (starting with book #30). Additionally, he's the author of **TAC Leader-What Honor Requires**, **Sarge, What Now?**, **Grandfather Speaks** and **Anderson's Rules**.

Bob is a qualified rappel master, holds a 2nd degree black belt in karate, and is an expert in weaponry and military tactics. He and his wife Pamela reside in Missouri.

To find out more about Bob Anderson or his books, or to inquire about having him speak at your next event, visit:

www.BobAndersonBooks.com

For more information
visit: www.speakingvolumes.us

Sign up for free and bargain books

Join the Speaking Volumes
mailing list

Text

ILOVEBOOKS

to 22828 to get started.

Message and data rates may apply